HiCK

andrea portes

Unbridled Books

Unbridled Books
Denver, Colorado

Library of Congress Cataloging-in-Publication Data

Portes, Andrea.
Hick / Andrea Portes.
p. cm.
ISBN-13: 978-1-932961-32-4
ISBN-10: 1-932961-32-1
[1. Runaways—Fiction.   2. Family problems—Fiction.   3. Coming of age—Fiction.   4. Swindlers and swindling—Fiction.   5. Sex—Fiction.   6. Automobile travel—Fiction.]   I. Title.

PZ7.P83615Hic 2007
[Fic]—dc22
2007000105

1   3   5   7   9   10   8   6   4   2

Book design by SH · CV

First Printing

for mom

"There never was such a country for wandering liars. . . ."

Mark Twain

ONE

Y ou know why you keep losing, cause, guess what, you're a fucking loser."

If I could grab you out your seat and make you fly past yourself and set you down in the middle of this red wooden shoebox, you'd be staring at my mama. You can see her now, ruddy-faced and getting a little too loud, some kind of aging Brigitte Bardot, ten years later and twenty pounds past what might have been, sitting there in a yellow tank, pink nails and blond flip-up hair. And the shoes, the shoes are the crowning glory, the angel on top of the tinsel tree, yellow plastic mules with a flower etched on the strap, just above her chipped pink toe-berries. My mama's littlest toe looks like a shrimp. She's half in the bag and not caring about bra strap showing or big brass laughing or acting slutty.

That's my dad, there in the corner, hunched over the bar like some kind of beaten question mark. He's staring fixed into his 7 & 7. Seven for give up. Seven for make do. Not much left over. There's no doubt in my mind that if he could dive headfirst into the ice-cube clinking whiskey pool dangling at the end of his fingertips, he would.

If you threw Elvis and a scarecrow in a blender, topped the whole thing off with Seagram's 7 and pressed dice, you would make my dad. He's got tar black hair and shoulder blades that cut through his undershirt like clipped wings. He looks like a gray-skinned, skinny-rat cowboy and I would be lying if I didn't say that I am, maybe sorta kinda, keep it secret, in love with him.

And you would be, too, you would, if you met him before drink number five or six. Just meet him then. Get lost before things get ugly.

His name is Nick, but call him Nicholas, like that Russian royal from my yard-sale World Book, cause if anybody in Lancaster County looks like some displaced king, it's my dad, shot through time like a diamond in a dirtbox.

My mama's name is Tammy, last name Cutter. And the worst part about it is, my dad can't stop being in love with her. Even as she sharpens her knife on the bones sticking out his back, even as she slurs her words, even as she makes goo-goo eyes at strangers, even then, he tilts his glass and shrugs and jiggles the change in his pocket and waits for her to love him back.

"I mean, they never win. They never win. Tom Osborne is just not a winning coach."

She lowers her voice to a loud and confidential whisper.

"I mean, if you ask me, he's just a dud. Just an old dud. He's not hungry enough to win."

And then, like she's gonna show you what true hunger looks like, she throws her head back, sucks down the rest of her berry-lime cooler and slams the empty glass on the bar like a drunk German, itching for a fight.

If you want to know how to reach us, you can call us here. Let's just say that's your best shot. So, here's the number, just ask for Nick. Let's just say the phone may or may not be working back home. Let's just say next to the line marked O for office, you can just put down the Alibi and Bob's your uncle. If you want to track us down on foot, it's that red neon sign three miles outside Lincoln, halfway down Highway 34 towards Palmyra. If you get to the water tower, you passed it.

"I hear they're gonna build a mall down on Route 5, cross from the slaughterhouse."

The bartender's trying to save me from hanging my head down and memorizing the floorboards. His name is Ray and he's known me since I was tall enough to put a quarter in the jukebox. The angels played a trick on him, giving him the body of a linebacker, then putting freckles all over him and topping the whole thing off with strawberry-blond hair. It's like if Strawberry Shortcake had a big brother that looked like he wanted to kick your ass.

Sometimes I call him Uncle Ray because sometimes he's the only one that makes sure I get home safe at night. He and I are in a secret club cause we both know the rest of the night by heart. We've watched this little drama played out, night after night, season by season, and Dad and Tammy are the stars of the show. That's the way it's gotta be, she wouldn't have it any other way. She's not stepping out of bed for just some two-line bit part.

Here's what's gonna happen. The little round glasses are gonna get filled and drained, filled and drained, over and over and over again. For about the first two drinks there's gonna be a nice breeze going through, simple, easy, light FM, lemonade by the side of the road.

Then around drink number three or four, everybody's gonna start having the time of their life. These guys are all gonna be best friends for good with everybody, that's for sure. Somebody is gonna play "That's Life" on the juke-box and everybody is gonna sing along and pat each other on the back and next thing you know, we're all moving in together.

Lord knows, "That's Life" is the anthem of drunks everywhere. If you want to make friends, just walk into any bar from here to Wahoo, find the juke-box, put in a quarter, play "That's Life" and watch the souses slur and sway. Before you know it those gin-blossom faces will be sidled-up, just a little too close, going on six ways till sundown, about the one that got away.

But wait till drink number three or four. That's when a fella could drop by from Timbuktu and be taken in as a brother, no matter what color or language or creed, we are all compadres here. He could be a Hatfield and the McCoys would sell him their sisters and offer him grits. Mi casa es tu casa. Mi bar es tu bar. Drinks are on me, amigos.

Then, around drink number five, everything is gonna get real quiet. I call this the calm before the storm. That is, when I call it anything, which is never, since the whole thing is so shamey, why talk about it in the first place? Why even mention it at all? Maybe let's just talk about the weather or the new mall down on Route 5.

Okay, now, here comes drink number six, that's a doozey. That's really the party crasher, that one. He comes in and you know there's gonna be trouble. You can hear the record scratch right when he walks through the door. Drink number six. Hold on to your hats.

Get out now, before drink number seven or eight come waltzing through the door, cause you can slice up the air with a butter knife. You can almost see the surliness rising up through the smoke, coming off the pool table. You could just tell drink number seven and eight to stay home, but they got invited with drink number one and they RSVP'd around drink number four. There is no way they are not coming to this party. They've been gussyed-up since happy hour.

So, here they are, drink number seven and eight, and here's Tammy, starting the show off with a bang.

"Luli, you're doomed, you know that. You are just fuckin doomed."

She's leaning in, serious, trying to get it through my head that this is the most important thing I ever heard ever. The words are dragging the side of her lip down, clumsy and falling slurred. She leers tipsy at my dad. If she could find a way to take back time by slicing up pieces off her husband, if she could turn his skin inside out and get a rebate, then she would cut and cut and not stop cutting until she's deep into the bone and even then. She would slice and dice with pleasure.

"I mean . . . look at this drunk you got for a dad, Luli. Lookit him. Just lookit him."

My mama likes to call my dad a drunk but she's giving him a run for his money. He's gonna sit in silence for a little while. He's gonna sit there and clink the ice in his whiskey and nod and drain his glass and drain another. It's gonna be a one-sided argument until he gets to drink number nine. That's when the fireworks start.

Here's what the argument is tonight. Tammy wants to go home. She doesn't want to be with a drunk like my dad no more, just lookit him. He doesn't want to leave. He's perfectly content with drink number nine and is starting to get a crush on drink number ten. Drink number ten has been batting her eyes at him for the last five minutes and my dad just can't resist. He's no match for that drink number ten. Her demure charms and mysterious ways are like a tonic. Like a gin and tonic.

"I am not gonna jus sit here night after night," Tammy says, "watchin my life pass me by, watchin you, lookin at you, thinkin that looky here what I got. This is the horse I bet on. Ha ha. That's a good one. That is precious."

None of this is new. This is like a script you'd follow if you were a vacuum-cleaner salesman. It's automatic. Instant. Standard practice.

My dad slams down drink number ten. I guess number ten was just a fling, cause he's out the door before the glass hits the bar. He's out the door now, storming through the gravel towards the sky-blue Nova parked always, forever, in the corner of the dirt lot. He's in that car and starting it up before you can say DUI.

I'm rushing along, trying to catch up, hoping this won't be the night, please God, not this night, not this one, when my dad finally acts out his final, inevitable, scene. It's the scene he's been writing for himself for years. I can practically hear the music swell up from the car wrapped around that old oak on Highway 34. The sound of the horn, drone drone, as the headlights cut into the pitch-black nothing and my dad's head turns the windshield into a glass spider web.

Not tonight. Please God, not tonight.

I'm almost to him by the time Tammy comes barreling past me on the left. He's trying to back up, but before he can she grabs the driver's side handle and wrenches the door open. She lurches in and throws herself over him, trying to grab the keys.

"You ain't driving nowhere like that, you sonuvabitch."

Oh, Lord, here we go.

"Tammy. You just shut the door, now. Just shut the door."

You'd never know he's on drink number ten now, cause that's how he gets. Calm. Quiet. Collected. My mama is maybe not so collected.

"You sonuvabitch, you ain't leavin me to raise Luli by myself, you selfish bastard."

This is when my dad remembers that he has a daughter and that, guess what, there I am. Just right there, smack-dab in the middle of the parking lot, standing dumb.

"Luli, get in the car. Get in the car now and we'll just leave your mama here. She's hysterical."

Now, that does it. Tammy throws hers arms around me like a spider devouring a fly and next thing you know she's protecting me like my life depended on it. This is her showstopper, ladies and gentlemen. This is where she brings down the house.

"Noooo. No. Nooo. You are not killing my daughter tonight. No sir. You are not takin my daughter with you. She's the only thing I have. My pride and joy."

She starts sobbing now. Make no mistake, this here is her show.

"Oh, Luli, Luli, I jus wanna do right by you. I do. I know your dad just, just can't hold down a job, just never could do nothin. I never shoulda married him, Luli. It's my fault. It's my fault. Blame me."

Now she is sobbing to beat the band. She did plays in high school and this is what it comes down to, drunken confessions in a square dirt lot.

"Luli, get in the car."

The song and dance tonight is called, "Who gets Luli?", followed by a little ditty of tears, followed by a fine little number about apologies, complete with sparkly smiles and a flourish of "I'll-never-do-it-again-I-promise."

Until the next show.

Now my dad is out the car and it's an all-out brawl. There might as well be banjo music. She's got my body, hunched over me like an old-fashioned vampire, nails digging little C's into my back. He's got my arm, pulling the both of us millimeter by millimeter to the car. This show's a comedy and we'll all be back next week.

We stay in this little clumsy tug-of-war for half a century, him pulling her, her clutching me, me trying to wriggle out, until all the sudden I feel two hands whisk me out and place me square four feet away.

"What the fuck is wrong with you people?"

It's Ray. He must've been waiting in the wings. He's got me beside him, holding his arm in front, protective. I wish he wouldn't wait so long to make his entrance. He almost missed his cue. The light from the bar cuts a rectangle into the gravel as the dust settles. There's a lot of huffing and puffing now.

"Look at yourselves. Jesus."

Tammy and Dad stand there like two kids caught smoking. They stand there, side by side, waiting for the next line, cooling down. But somehow the shame thrown down missed them and hit me direct. They're just trying to straighten their shirts. They're just trying to figure out the most perfect closing line to get them the fuck offstage.

"C'mon, Luli," Ray says. "I'll give you a ride home. I'm sorry. I am truly sorry."

He puts his hand on my shoulder and takes me with him while he tells the bar-back to cover, quick. He doesn't want nothing to do with this show no more. He's had it. There's nothing grand or loud or pretty about the way he steers me across the gravel. There's nothing flashy about the way he hoists me up into the truck, deep red, with giant wheels for winter. He just sets me up top the seat, simple, before strutting around and getting in the driver's side. He starts the engine and pulls out the lot, with not even a wink back to remind us he's the hero.

When we're pulling out onto Highway 34, I look back and see my dad leaning on the hood of the Nova. You could practice for years and never lean with that picture perfect cowboy slunk.

And you would think that would be it and call it a night, I bet. But just wait cause two fence-posts past our drive Ray stops the truck and next thing you know I'm staring into the big black night with just two headlights, that's it for miles. He starts mumbling something about there's a funny noise he's gotta check up on and there I am, feet up on the dash, thumb-twiddling.

If you're wondering what I look like, just throw two giant eyes and one big mouth at a face too small to hold them. There must've been a mix-up that day on the assembly line, cause they got the proportions all wrong. I got made fun of for my big mouth before I even made it to day-care. Fish-face. Quacky-duck. Put it on my bill.

Seems like Ray's doing a whole lot of nothing, tinkering with the engine and grunt grunt grunt but then, next thing you know, he's got his head in my window like he's the weatherman on the nightly news.

"Wull. I can't figure it."

"Figure what?"

"The noise. I can't figure the noise."

"Huh."

"Look, Luli."

Now he starts scratching the back of his neck, shifting leg to leg.

"I wanna show you something."

Boy, he sure knows how to be boring.

Shift. Shift.

"Wull, what?"

Shift.

"Um, wull, how bout you close your eyes and open your mouth."

"Wull, why would I wanna do that?"

"Just trust me. Trust me. You'll like it. I promise."

And now something in the air around me starts to vibrate and I get the feeling that funny noise was pure make-up and my thumbs stop mid-twiddle.

But there's also a side of me that won't ever look away from a dead bird or a car chase or a hold-up at the Alibi at 2 a.m. There's this side that wants to grab that buzzing thing and pull it close and twirl it around and inspect it, like dissecting a frog, belly-splayed.

So I do it.

I do what he says and I close my eyes and open my mouth and the next thing I know he's got his twenty-eight-year-old tongue in my thirteen-year-old mouth and all I can think is that I don't think the hero is supposed to be doing this.

He was supposed to grab me out the hullabaloo and gallop me off on a palomino horse, straight up into Orion's Belt and up up up into the stars. Just leave out the step about making up truck noises and grumbling round the tires and then he's got his tongue down my throat. Don't tell that part. That part's double-secret.

I squirm away and look at him like his marbles got lost. He looks at me, eyes swirling, and get this.

That thing swirling in his eyes, that thing, like he wants to jump into my body and devour me from the inside out, makes it like I could ask for whatever my little heart desired in this second and he would have to do it. He wouldn't have a choice. Right here, in this second in the dead black night with nothing but two white beams and a fence-post waning, I could ask him to climb Chimney Rock or go rob a bank or take me to Lincoln, no, Omaha, no, Dallas. I could ask him, in this little speck of a moment, to jump off a cliff or spit on his mama or crash his truck into the Missouri and he'd do it. He'd have to do it.

And I don't know if it's the way I open my eyes or the way I gawk at his eyes swirling, but he steps back and looks at the ground and shuffles his feet and shakes his head. Then he gets back over to the driver's seat, real quick.

Silent. Silent.

Two fence-posts back.

Silent.

Down the drive.

Silent.

Slam the door.

Silent.

Not even a good-bye. No sir. Not now.

And as I watch him crunching over the gravel, kicking up dust down the drive and into the nothing black night, I could jump for joy.

I could jump for joy, cause now I know I've got something. Fish-face. Quacky-duck's got something. I've got something that cancels out too-broke Dad and cancels out dirt-lot brawls and cancels out that leaning, falling house I'm about to walk into. I got something that's gonna throw me straight into the sun and leave this shitty little dust-bin behind and you just wait, you just wait, to see how I make it go boom.

TWO

Did you know I have a baby brother? Had one. It's cause Tammy had a blue dress. Tammy had a baby-blue dress that came down not far enough and my dad liked her in that blue dress and then, the next thing you know, that blue dress started fitting tighter and tighter around her belly and, next thing you know, it looked like she swallowed a basketball and, next thing you know, my dad was skipping around talking about, "Luli, you're gonna have a little baby brother, now, you're gonna have to help your mama now, see."

And even though I was only seven and didn't know why Tammy swallowed a basketball or how that made a baby brother, you couldn't help but smile when you saw my dad floating through the door and through the next, sashaying around Mama in her too-tight blue dress. And she'd say, "Now, c'mon, now, you don't know it's gonna be a boy, you just don't know that, just shush." And he'd say, "Yes, I do. I do sure know it like I know the sky is blue and I know the world is round and I know I married the most beautiful girl in the county, the state, the whole wide world, darlin, the whole big wide world."

And this is the part where he'd sidle up behind her and start rocking back and forth and making her blush and play-swat him away, but she's swaying, too, swaying there in that baby-blue dress, too.

And they had a Sunday with everyone coming over and bringing gifts and a cake and a little baby crib from Aunt Gina and Uncle Nipper, white with gold trim, like something you pulled out of a dollhouse and blew up life-size. And they were laughing and giggling and smiling thirty ways till sundown. And you would have been smiling, too, cause it was like all the good-mornings and all the hi-how-are-yas and all the well-hello-sunshines in the county had taken lunch all at once and decided to march down the dirt road and alight, just this once, just this one Sunday afternoon, and arrange themselves in a circle around my basketball-swallowing mama, sitting proud and pretty in that blue dress that started it all.

And maybe God and the angels took note of that blue dress, too, because when that baby came out the color of moonlight, we all knew something was wrong.

And he was a boy, all right, Dad got that part right, but he wasn't the kind of boy you could take out front and throw a football to in four years or five or even six. No, sir, he was just born the color coming off the moon and sickly and sniffling and stiff. He was just born with a frown on his face, like he got dropped off at the wrong planet or maybe the angels left out a step or maybe he didn't want nothing to do with it in the first place.

And he had to set in that incubator like some kind of other-world baby chick while my dad and Aunt Gina and Uncle Nipper just waited and waited and whispered and whispered and spent more and more money they didn't have in the first place, just to keep him down on this here planet.

And there was a doctor came in from Omaha and he took one look at that baby and said we best be bringing him up there, cause that's where they've got the best doctors and the best treatment money can buy, and my dad smiled and nodded and said oh-yes-Doctor, and that baby stayed right there in that incubator for three days straight before deciding that maybe this wasn't the place for him after all. Maybe this wasn't the right planet or the right county or the right too-broke family from somewhere out in the sticks, anyways, and so he just upped and took to floating back up into the blue sky from whence he came, back up to wherever planet you get to go to when you get born the color of moonlight and your too-poor daddy can't afford to send you up to Omaha, where they've got the best white-coated smiling doctors that know what the fuck to do anyways.

You see, it's one thing to pretend you're James Dean and pump gas in the summer and make the girls blush before heading back to your double-wide. It's one thing to pack mules in the fall and live in a log cabin and dip your hat down before riding off into the setting sun. But when not being able to scrape two dimes together makes it so your baby boy, born the color of the night sky, has to stay put in that glowing tin-cup incubator instead of up with the experts in Omaha, well, then, there's nothing glamorous about that, now, is there?

And she didn't have to say it, my mama, when the bones fell out her body all at once and Aunt Gina and Uncle Nipper tried to hold her rag-doll body up by the elbows. She didn't have to say it, my mama, when it was like God himself had his heel into her back, holding her head down into the linoleum. She didn't have to say it, my mama, when my dad tried to shush her sobbing into the tile, when she pulled back, recoiled at just even the inkling, the beginning, the thought of his hand on her arm. She didn't have to say it. None of it. We all knew. We all knew.

And Uncle Nipper knew to go to the house and get rid of that white crib with gold trim, before Mama could set eyes on it, please Lord, just do it. And Aunt Gina knew to take that baby-blue dress and just bury it, bury it deep in the back of her closet far, far away, before Sunday visits and swallowing basketballs and boys born the color coming off the moon. And I knew, this is when I first knew, this is when I learned how to throw myself over to the other side of the room and watch my dumb little life like I was watching a movie and you get the popcorn and we'll sit a spell and see what else goes by.

And there goes Dad, he's been slumping around for three weeks straight with his head hanging off his shoulders. And there goes Mama, she still can't eat but bring her this macaroni salad, just in case. And there goes most of my little-kid playmates, cause no one wants a fucking thing to do with this house anymore, that's for damn sure. And here comes Aunt Gina and Uncle Nipper with a few kind words and making sure I got at least some Malt-O-Meal and Chef Boyardee to tide me over, they'll be back tomorrow. And there goes my baby blue brother, somewhere into the night sky above me, and I wonder if I get to see him someday and tell him about the white crib he missed out on and that I know it wasn't much but we were real proud to have him and wanted him to stay, just wanted him to stay a spell, and I would have played whatever silly little dumb game he had in mind, really, I was just happy to have him, my baby brother born the color of dusk.

And you better just learn to throw yourself twenty feet across the room and let it play, just let it play. You better just learn to put each day and night up onto that screen and just keep on watching. Here's what you'll see. You get to see the incredible shrinking man. You get to see a man six foot tall turn in on himself and slump forward into nothing and then gone. Poof. You get to see a great tale of revenge and lust with a beautiful blond with flip-up hair. You get to see her get gussyed up each evening and put on lipstick and giggle loud and bat her eyelashes at strangers, straying a little bit behind the Alibi on a Saturday night, no, better, make that Sunday. Hell, she might run off with the devil himself if he walked in, leaned his elbow on the jukebox and tipped his hat just so.

You get to see all these attractions and then some. You get to see Elvis-style dreamboats and slutted-up little girls and eyes swirling wild by the side of the road. You get to see naughty pink parts and coming attractions and wait, just wait, there's more, keep watching, keep watching, let it play, let it play.

THREE

People think we're poor but I made a list of things we have, just to set them straight.

We have one seventy-year-old farmhouse, complete with barn, shack and an acre of tall wheat with weeds sticking up. We have all this luxury thanks to my grandpa who gave it to my mama when he died, on account of she was marrying a no good, ne'er-gonna-make-nothing-out-of-his-skinny-bone-self like my dad. Despite the fact that it is, at first glance, a farmhouse, we don't farm it or anything like that. We wouldn't even know where to start. Tammy's been trying to grow an avocado tree out of a pit for three years.

All told, we got a yellow farmhouse and a green barn and a blue shack but they're all faded to about the same color anyways. The paint's cracked and the wood on each of these little monuments that make up our own private village is washed out to gray, light gray, gray-blue or dark gray. The barn has a huge loft in it full of hay and smelling like horses, even though there haven't been horses here for twenty years. Just about the only animal life in there are the bats that flutter around thirty feet up top the loft making it Halloween all year round.

It's so thick with cobwebs up there I'm surprised the bats don't get caught and eaten up by some imaginary spider of hideous proportion with sinister, darting eyes. On the other side of the cobwebs, facing out into the wheat dusk air, is a white-circle silhouette of a horse centered on each side of the barn, staring proud off into the setting sun.

In front of the barn is our humble abode, which is faded yellow inside and out, with tiny-blue-flower wallpaper on a white-and-gold background in both the entry, which we never use, and the dining room, which we use even less. Everything in our rickety faded buttercup house, dead straight across from the biggest cemetery in Lancaster County, built around 1910, for the gravedigger and his wife, actually still runs properly, with the one exception of some hullabaloo about the water.

Some orange-vested worker men from Lincoln came out here a few years back, noodled with the well tap and warned us that we had too much lithium in our water, declaring that it'd be best for everyone if we just relocated. This is something we never did, of course, because we didn't have nowhere to relocate to, and Mama says, "Shit, wull, if we have lithium in our water we might as well see it as some kinda healing bonus and make the best of it . . . some people might even pay extra for that."

Sides all that, we got one RCA color TV with wood on the sides and that sky blue Chevy Nova my dad takes pride in scurrying around and underneath on weekends, fixing and tinkering and muttering to himself about trannies, alignment and pistons.

And I know that these things may not seem like much to some la-di-da snooty-pants from Omaha but there are plenty of people in Lancaster County who have less than that, so I know, for a fact, that we're not poor.

Okay, this is what there is. Sometimes there's macaroni and cheese, with tuna, for protein, but that's pretty much as good as it gets. If you're still hungry you can have blue frosting on graham crackers for dessert. There's also the option, sometimes, of a sugar sandwich, which involves two slices of white bread, buttered thick and spread with plain white sugar. And then other times, depending on how many days my dad's been gone, there's even the possibility of me just stealing our dinner from the Piggly Wiggly in Fremont or Wahoo or Alliance in case it's a special occasion . . . birthday, Christmas, Easter . . . usually something involving ham. Ham means it's a holiday and wear a shirt.

Tammy did a fairly reasonable job of teaching me how to steal when I was ten, but the knack I have for it comes mostly from my last three years of experience and has little to do with her slightly naive take on shopkeepers and advantage-taking. You may be thinking, oh my good Lord, what kind of a mother would put her own offspring up to such mischief and certain jeopardy? But, in all actuality, there's a trick to it.

You see, this way, if I get caught, she can scold me and pretend like she's so ashamed, she raised me with the Lord Jesus Christ in my heart and how could I betray her, the baby Jesus and the blessed Virgin Mary like that. Believe me, she knows how to showboat.

By the end of it, she'd have the shopkeeper so caught up in his own journey, or lack of journey, towards Jesus Christ our Lord and

Savior that they'd just go ahead and let us go. They'd be too busy feeling sorry for me that I had such a pious mama that was surely going to spend this lifetime and the next dragging me through fire and brimstone before flying up to heaven on a puffy Charmin cloud.

I am proud to say that, with the help of Jesus Christ and the Bible, I've stolen our special-occasion family dinner for three years straight and not once had to face up to any power higher than the day clerk at the Piggly Wiggly.

It's the little things like that I try to think about when I know I'm about to start feeling sorry for myself in my little yellow house with my stupid life and nothing to eat.

Lookit, if you think you can just march out to the kitchen and say a fine howdedoo this morning, you got another thing coming, that's for damn sure. No sir, here's how it's got to be if you know what's good for you. Peek. Tippy-toe. Tippy-toe. Down the hall. Peek. Tippy-toe. Tippy-toe. Down the kitchen. Peek. Investigate the ashtray. You can read that ashtray like a weather-vane.

You know how most people turn on the TV to figure out the weather and how the day's gonna turn out? Well, round here the ashtray is gonna tell you who's three sheets to the wind and if the storm's rolling in or already passed. You best learn to read it if you know what's good for you.

Empty ashtray means partly sunny. Empty ashtray means the coast is clear. Go about your day. Nothing to see here.

Full ashtray ain't bad either. Full ashtray means the storm's passed. Don't worry. They're all in bed now, it's over. Just hope for full or empty ashtray.

Full ashtray with lit cigarette?

Well, you can't win em all. That lit cigarette means the storm's rolling in. Brace yourself.

Now, if you think that's bad, just wait till you find a full ashtray with *more than one* lit cigarette. That is the last thing you want to see. If there's more than one lit cigarette in that ashtray, you might as well tippy-toe back down the hall, pull the covers over your head, huddle and wait out the storm. More than three lit cigarettes in that ashtray and you best evacuate. More than three cigarettes means it's gonna be a doozey. Hold on tight. Category 5.

Look here, it's bad enough if you get one lit cigarette. That means the night before got piggy-backed over into this morning and the drinks are still going strong. They could be out there carousing with drink number eight to thirteen, for God's sake. Who's even counting anymore anyways? Might as well just drink out the bottle.

But if you get more than three lit cigarettes in that thing, that means Dad corralled some barflies over in a fit of generosity, probably somewhere near the third chorus of "That's Life." Hey, folks, let's go to my place, we're all amigos here.

They'll be sitting there, round the kitchen table, unwitting, smoke coming up off their fingers, dazzled by my dad. Sitting ducks. He'll be telling them all about that day he got stuck in the mud down by Wahoo and then this happened and then that happened and can you believe he got out, no one thought he could. They'll be in love with him just like I am, just like Tammy used to be. They'll be thinking this guy is the greatest guy since sliced bread, that's for sure. If there's a lady in the crowd, she'll be thinking bout how she can sidle up to him on the way to the bathroom, maybe. She'll be checking her lipstick and hiking up her bra every time he looks away. She's got plans for him. Big plans.

They'll never see it coming. No sir. I almost feel sorry for them, smiling dumb round that ashtray. They don't know that drink number eight or nine are gonna be dropping by soon, looking for a brawl. They don't know they've got a date with drink number ten that involves a lot of hollering, throwing bottles and knocking that front door off its hinges. They got no idea. That front door has been slammed off its hinges so many times we haven't even bothered to put it back since June.

Maybe tomorrow.

But this morning I am breathing a sigh of relief because that ashtray is empty, thank God. Bout time we had a little peace and quiet around here.

There is one little thing wrong with the kitchen, though, at present, which is that there happens to be a man in a gray suit sitting smack-dab in the middle of it. That's a new one.

It's not that a beaten-up farmhouse ten minutes outside of Palmyra, Nebraska, is an especially dangerous place to be, but it has happened. Twenty minutes east of here, in Alliance, there was a whole family got shot in cold blood about five years back. Two guys from Dodge sashayed into town, walked in, lined all four of them up on the floor and fired, but not until each of them had taken a turn with their fourteen-year-old daughter who happened to be runner-up Modern Miss Teenage Nebraska.

She was wearing a light-blue nightgown when it happened and in the pictures of the aftermath it looked like it had a flower pattern on it from all the blood, dark-brown and red flowers, abstract and huge. The blood down the inside of her legs was crackled and dried up into little pieces. Her eyes were wide open and she looked like a shattered doll.

Not me.

I slink back to my room and get something girls aren't supposed to have but I do. Uncle Nipper gave it to me for my thirteenth birthday, along with a T-shirt that says, "Take Me Drunk I'm Home." It's a cockroach colored .45 and just looking at it makes you feel mean. It looks bad and looks like it'll bring bad with it.

It's my pride and joy.

I got some hot moves I picked up from Clint Eastwood and here's my chance. I must have practiced this scene ten times since my birthday. Watch me sidle down the hall, hugging the wall, eyes froze. Make him turn around first. That's what Clint would do. You gotta wait till they see you and make yourself big. You gotta show them your soul got left back, long ago, before handing them their walking papers from this shiny life to the next.

He's sitting at the head of the table like he owns the place. His back is towards me and his neck is just waiting there like a baked potato for me to take aim. His head shimmers, bald and stubbly, with a few moles here and there like towns spread out in Oklahoma. He's got a briefcase on his lap, proper-like. There's something in the way he's holding his chin up or maybe it's the slope of his nose that tells me he's got money and that this place, my place, might as well be the outhouse outside a cathouse.

I prop myself up in the doorway, leaning slight to the side, making sure to hold the .45 real casual. I turn myself mean inside out, freeze my skin and say, "That's my dad's chair."

His knee knocks up the table and he turns round, flustered and blustery. I could jump for joy, I really could, he looks like such an idiot, but instead I choose to concentrate on my intimidating tactics. Clint wouldn't jump for joy.

"Well, my oh my, you sure gave me a scare."

He pretends not to see my .45, reflecting around the room, whirling slowly in little bright circles that can only spell his doom. He nervous smiles but I don't smile back. I just stare at him and raise my chin a little.

"Is your mother home?"

"Nope."

"Do you know when she'll be back?"

"Nope."

"Do you know where she went?"

"Nope."

"Do you always carry a gun like that?"

"Yep."

"That's a very, um, nice gun."

"What gun?"

"That gun. It's . . . interesting."

"My gun is interesting?"

"Well, I mean, it seems to be very well crafted."

"It's not a gun. It's a .45."

"Um."

"Smith and Wesson."

"Maybe I could give you my card and you could tell her I dropped by . . . "

"Card?"

"Yes. Um. Here."

He smiles and takes his card out. He reaches his arm towards me and dangles it out for me to grab. I don't move.

"Who are you, Mister?"

"Oh, I'm sorry. How rude of me. My name's Lux. Lux Feld. I'm in investments."

"Investments?"

"You know, land, property, stuff like that."

He laughs light and shrugs, making nice. I nod and laugh light back, shuffling my feet against the linoleum floor and slapping my thigh like I'm the inbred retard he takes me for.

He stops laughing and puts his card back in his jacket.

"You always break into people's houses at . . . what time is it?"

"Eight o'clock."

"At 8 o'clock in the morning?"

"Well, actually, the door was open, er, there was no door, I mean a screen door but . . . you know, well, I'm sorry, I didn't see a buzzer so I just thought I'd—"

"Do you think I'm pretty?"

"Excuse me?"

"Do you think I'm pretty? Like if you saw me passing by would you want to kiss me or something?"

"Um. I don't really think that's—"

"Luli, what the hell are you doing?"

Tammy comes barreling down the staircase, pushing me aside, and I can tell she's about to do something worse but then she sees Mr. Feld and it's like she turns from a moth to a butterfly in two seconds flat. She straightens up and tightens her robe around her, fluffing her hair up and smiling pretty.

"Why, Mr. Feld. Whatever in the world are you doing here at this hour of the day, of the morning, I mean? It must be seven-thirty, seven even."

"It's actually eight, Mrs. Cutter."

He looks at her kind of funny when he says her name, like there's a little joke here they got between them. They're both smiling now. Tammy starts looking a little red like she's at the sock-hop. And I have seen this blushing before. It means my dad is on the outs again.

I'm surprised this mister is even talking to her looking like that, sunk-eyed and shabby in her frayed blue robe and last night's makeup. She keeps adjusting and readjusting herself, like somewhere in the position of her belt lies true happiness.

"I mean, I wouldn't even have woke up if it wasn't for Luli and her loud laughing."

She looks at me for that one. I smile back at her like I'm just as happy as she is and we're all just one big happy family. She sees my .45 and grabs it out of my hand.

"Oh, Luli, you are just such a little card with that gun."

She laughs, bashful, swatting her hand at Mr. Feld, covering.

"She don't mean nothing. She just likes to play."

"It's not a gun. It's a .45." I repeat it, get it straight.

"Well, that's nice, dear."

Tammy smiles and the peeled worm takes a gulp.

"Okay, then, Mr. Feld, if you'll just let me get dressed, I'll be right back down."

She turns my way and smiles like a TV commercial.

"Luli, you better start getting ready for school now."

All smiles. New and improved soap.

"School don't start for two weeks."

She grabs my arm and steers me firm towards my room. I look back at her and she stares right back like she's daring me to make a move. Tammy's got a mean backhand. I turn and start getting dressed, careful to stand next to the door so I can keep up. I hear her sigh and giggle, then a little laughing and talking. A guilty little whisper. A sentence, hushed.

Then the screen door slams and just like that they're gone.

I walk back out to the kitchen and listen to the sound of a smooth kind of car driving off into the distance. Well, that's that then. If my calculations are correct, he's not new to her cause there's already a secret between them. She must have found him at the Hy-Vee or the Kwik-Mart or the Piggly Wiggly. He must have driven his cart into her cart, blushed and feigned an apology, polite. She would have turned round, seen money and they'd be off to the races.

Money.

I open the fridge for something to eat, but there's nothing but brown peaches and a half-finished jar of relish.

I bet this morning my mama gets bacon and eggs with waffles on the side.

I look through the rest of the cupboards, clacking away, quicker and quicker, until some Saltines make their way into my hands and up to my mouth, stale.

Upstairs I hear the sound of my dad stirring.

I settle down into the chair, collected. He walks down the staircase and squints at me through the doorway.

"Where's your mother?"

"She left."

"With who?"

"Somebody."

"Somebody who?"

"Some guy."

Something changes in the whiskey sweat air around him. He freezes and gets a little taller altogether, shrinking and getting bigger in the same miracle breath. He looks at the wallpaper like he can see right through it, all the way to wherever and whatever that fancy car has driven off to.

"His name's Lux. He's kinda gay."

"By gay do you mean that he's a homosexual?"

"I don't know."

"Wull, some folks don't like that word, so you should find a new one."

"Like what?"

"I dunno, something sweet. You're a girl, girls supposed to be sweet."

Then he looks at what I'm wearing. Not much.

"You wearing that outta the house?"

"Maybe, why, what's wrong with it?"

"Seems a little light on the clothing part, don't you think?"

"Wull, what do you think?"

"I think you look like trouble."

"Wull, I can change, I guess—"

"No use lookin for trouble, Luli, it'll find you soon enough."

He looks at me there, staring up at him from the foot of the staircase, and something strange and wistful takes over his face.

"You know, it's funny . . . in this light . . . you look just like your mother when I first met her . . . just blond and pretty . . . before she got mean."

I look up at him, wanting to tell him I'm sorry, wanting to fix him and make him hate her back.

"Don't get mean, Luli, just stay little and pretty and sweet, how bout that?"

I try to make my face smile but I think I'm turning out more of a grimace, some little girl squint into the sunlight.

"Just stay sweet."

He stares at me like that for what seems like two weeks.

Then he snaps out of it like some broken spell, looking at me like I'm this demonic Muppet sent to hurl him into the abyss with trouble dressing and stray-cat luring.

"Tell your mama, when you see her, tell her I had some business myself, tell her I had some business out in Shelby and I may be gone for a while, you know . . . paperwork."

Paperwork.

Now I know that's a lie.

The last time I saw my dad pick up a pen, I was eight.

Then he barrels past me, quick, grabs his keys off the wall and rushes out the screen door, letting it slam hard behind. I go to the door and watch as he drives away, churning up dust all the way down the dirt road and into the horizon.

He doesn't look back.

FOUR

I wander off to the barn to consider my options. It's the day dying down, the hay and the wood smelling sweet and dusty. The grass and the heat of the day coming off the ground, up up up into the giant pink sky.

It may have been that word paperwork. It may have been the way the dust was flying up underneath the tires or the back side of the Nova as it shrunk into a glossy speck on the beige horizon, but something in my gut, sure as sugar, tells me this:

He ain't coming back.

Now I'm not trying to cry wolf, since I've been accused of some such shenanigans before, but I just know this as a fact in the back of my neck and the bottom of my belly. He won't be back. No way. Not after paperwork. I don't think I've ever seen my dad sign a check, let alone take a stab at paperwork.

There are some things you just know, like when the sun goes down and you know something different is gonna happen that night. You may not know what it is and it may not turn out to be much, but something in the air changing around you or the night creeping up tells you this time you're in for it.

I feel like that right now.

I've felt like that all day long and into the night, this night, that's holding something behind its back.

The second idea muddling its way up the back of my head and into focus stems from the way my frazzled, blue-robed mama was looking at that bald-headed man. It cannot be denied. She has it between the legs for him.

I don't know what he's got for her, if it's in his head or his heart or his wallet, but it doesn't really matter now, does it? Because he's got her. That's his problem. Good luck. Once Tammy gets her hooks into something or somebody it's hard to get her out or off or out of the picture. Like some kind of blond tick, she'll just suck and suck until she's swelled up with blood, sweat and tears, like a needy grape. Then she'll either burst, leaving your inside carnage strewn out about the kitchen floor, or she'll just hop off, casual-like, as if nothing ever happened.

You gotta watch her like that. See whether she'll bite or just hop off. The problem is, she has that blond flip, lipstick, I-can-make-your-dreams-come-true disguise that makes a fella forget his own name. I'd feel sorry for that old gray-suit peeled worm, if he hadn't come in, usurped my daddy and drove off with Tammy to money-land, without a glance backwards, through the dust. As it is, though, I've got my own problems to worry about.

My two conclusions lead me to a third and final one, which goes something like this:

My time for the next few weeks, months, maybe years is gonna be spent either alone, like right now, swinging my feet out the barn with a gurgling stomach, or, possibly, with Tammy and that peeled worm in wealthypeopleworld with a fake smile and a quickie in the closet and a coming out the pantry out of breath, belt-buckling.

And though you might think I ought to clap my hands together, shout hallelujah and thank God the money train has somehow seen fit to stop outside my door, you yourself would be on the wrong track. This is cause you yourself would not be thinking about watching blushing and backrooms and groping of your for-sale mama while your dad is somewhere two sheets to drunksville. Look, the rich get richer and the poor get the picture. That's what my daddy says and that is why I am not about to align myself on the mean side of Tammy's meandering.

So, as neither of these two possibilities strikes me as a satisfactory way to spend my first official year as an American girl teenager, I choose to opt for a third and final possibility that I'll call none of the above.

Now, let's get something straight here, this will not be easy and could easily end in disaster, jail and death. But all three of these sad conclusions, to my mind, sure beat staying here with a grumbling stomach, staring at myself in the mirror, looking at my mouth, lips, tits, knees, feet and between my legs, trying to figure out what the difference is between me and all those girls in the magazines, on the TV and in the movies. Because, even with my quacky bill, I am just as easy on the eyes as they are, and they all seem to be happy and glowing and rich, so why aren't I?

Lookit, there's got to be a way to turn that thing, that thing with swirling eyes, into three meals a day and not have to steal them. I saw what I saw and I'm gonna make it go.

See you could take it, you could take that thing, that thing that makes their eyes go round and you could turn it up and cash it in for a rebate and not have to eat cold beans for lunch and vow to never, never care about love or romance or soap-opera promises. You could just cash in on that eye swirl.

So that's it. I make up my mind to find a sugar-daddy who will fawn over me and feed me whenever I'm hungry, not just with sugar sandwiches but with rich-people food. He'll pour out different-flavored Riunites in different-shaped glasses and blather on about oak-barrels and rainfall and grapes. I'll say, It does go well with the fish, and smile, and he'll be proud and want to buy me more stuff. He'll take me shopping, watch me try on dresses and tell me he insists I get every one, even the red one. I'll say, Oh no I can't take this, but he'll say, Yes you can and throw in this necklace, too, while you're at it.

I'll try that out for a while, see how I like it. Although, now that I think about it, it's not going to be easy sitting in the middle of nowhere Nebraska looking for a leg up. We may have an abundance of shiftless ranch hands, but sugar-daddies are in short supply, no doubt about it. Nebraska is a poor state with poor people with nowhere to go and no hurry to get there.

No sir.

This is gonna take drastic action.

I weigh my options and realize I will have to head west. That's where they grow cowboys with ten-gallon hats and big skies with cactus and bright gold jewelry with turquoise and snakes.

West it is. I'll have to get out while the getting is good, before that gray-suit larva comes in and takes over, telling me what to do with some legal mumbo jumbo he learned in Lincoln. I do not want him doling out my chores while patting Tammy on the ass. That is for damn sure.

I'll have to find someplace shiny-like and mean, with rich people throwing money away like they're bragging by doing it. Someplace where I can sneak around the back sides of buildings, make my way with a smile and a few clever words, before striking. Someplace where there's people to fool worth fooling . . .

And then it hits me clear as day.

Las Vegas.

That's it, no question, no contest. Las Vegas, Nevada, where there's desert and gambling and lights and drinking all through the night with no one to know me or tell me what to do or get in the way of all my ingenious money-making schemes. I'll go there and make it mine, become one of the legends of the city, someone they talk about for years after, who came and went but no one really knew deep inside. They'll whisper about me in dark rooms late at night, a character of mystery and intrigue who was feared and respected throughout the city, out into the desert and the netherworld beyond.

I better bring something to dazzle them.

I'll need something that reeks of class and sophistication, like on Remington Steele. I burrow through Tammy's closet and come up with some expert disguises. My new life will be dangerous but full of glamour. I picture myself with the lights coming up behind me in Vegas. I see myself framed by the cowboy made of neon looming up glittery with the promise of knocking my socks off.

Except there's the issue of money. As fucking usual. But I'm way ahead on this one. Some mystery person, and I'm assuming it's my mama, has got two hundred smackers saved up in a crumple behind the trash can, under the kitchen sink. That's her brilliant idea of a secret. I found it by almost throwing it out. I figure it must be from that gray-suit peeled worm she's running around with. My dad ain't got money enough to bring home a box of Corn Pops, let alone two-hundred smackers. I guess Mr. Gray-Suit thinks he's providing for his future family, bought and paid for.

I wish I could see her face when she sees it's gone.

And now, last but not least, one fancy black bag I stole from this girl I hate. She belongs to the Knolls Country Club and has a habit of talking about it to everyone around her and inviting everyone in the class. Except me. I guess I'm not country club material. I guess I'm the girl with the ripped-up knee-socks and leftover clothes and an artichoke for lunch.

I get it.

Well, I took her bag and the only thing I regret is that I can't give it back and take it again. And ten years down the line she'll be begging me to be her country club guest and I'll remind her I'm just the Twinkie-raised girl with the ripped-up knee-socks, no thanks. You can get a nose job while I fuck your husband in the back.

So long, suckers.

Now I'm down the stairs and out the gate.

I always knew I would fly off someday. I just never knew when, sitting in the barn, swinging my legs out, waiting for the starter pistol behind my eardrums to go pop. But it never came. It sidled up and pondered and wishy-washed itself around my skull, playing some kinda chorus of not yet. But the pop pop never came. Until now, this moment, here, where all my fears and doubts and misgivings have come to the dance to ask my dreams for a whirl. And just as I know that my daddy is probably deep into the panhandle by now, way past Alliance and not looking back, I know that now, this, this moment here, is the pop pop pop.

I wonder what they'll say about me when I'm gone. I wonder how long it'll take them to figure out I ain't coming back. Just the thought of it makes me whistle and puts a zing in my shoe-step. I am not what they thought I was. No sir. I am bigger than this whole state put together and I have listened and I have waited and now I can hear it. Pop.

Here's where I turn and start walking down the gravel road. I feel like there's something coming up underneath my feet, something lifting me and moving me forward, something just waiting to throw me into the sun.

FIVE

Somewhere between Palmyra and Alliance, a beat-up green-and-white pick-up truck, with a gun rack in the back, pulls up behind me while I'm singing to myself. I look inside and there, in the driver's seat, sits a skinny bug-eyed cowboy who looks like a turtle. He looks like he must have spent the last ten days straight chasing squealers in the rodeo and hasn't changed since. He's got on one of them old fashioned Western shirts with a pattern of little rose flowers faded dingy into gray, mother-of-pearl snaps gleaming creamy in a line from his chest down to his jeans, untucked. He's got a look about him that you wouldn't be surprised if he just busted out of the nervous hospital.

He rolls down the window and shouts over the wind,

"Where you headed?"

"Las Vegas."

He looks me up and down.

"Aren't you a little bit young and maybe, say, innocent to be traveling to Las Vegas all by your little self?"

He's got this tone in his voice like he's got three friends snickering, hunkering down in the cab, and this is all a little joke between them.

"No." I straighten up a bit. "What about you, Mister? Where you headed?"

"Well, I don't see how that's any of your business . . . and my name's not Mister, it's Eddie. Eddie Kreezer."

I smile and make a bashful act, bending over myself, trying to let him sneak a peek at my newfound bubbles, hoping for a free ride. I figure I can turn his none-of-your-business into Las Vegas with a little bit of sugar. My age makes him nervous and shamey, cause his eyes keep heading southwards and then back up, guilty. I can tell I can make his eyes swirl and that's just about all I want to do.

"You some kinda runaway?"

"No. My dad ran away and left me."

This is my new version of my life story.

"Oh yeah?"

"Yeah. I guess he thought I could fend for myself, but I sure could use a ride, Mister, Eddie, and I'm just worried sick that I won't find a place to stay before dark and I guess I'm just plum scared and all cause—"

"What's your dad look like? Maybe I seen him." He takes off his hat and squints at the brim like he's inspecting it.

"You."

There is a silence as he looks me up and down. Then he just starts laughing, real hard and loud, like his make-believe friends just jumped out the back and the dashboard just turned into a bar.

"Oh my God, what in the world is in store for me here?" he says, shaking his head and smiling to himself. "Well, well, well . . ."

I don't really get his little private joke, but I smile anyways, not wanting to seem dumb or too young or rude even. I resolve to take the reins.

"You gonna give me a ride or are you just gonna sit there and laugh at yourself all day?"

He stops laughing.

"Oh, I get it, you're some kinda ten-year-old smart-ass or something."

"Try thirteen," I say, real smug.

"Well. You're just about old enough to have kids then, aren't ya?"

He sneers gritty through the corner of his mouth, like Uncle Nipper used to do when the ashtray says he's been up all night and the bottle of Jack confirms it with two sips left. For once in my life I am struck dumb for words and I don't like it. I shift my attention to the ground and shuffle my feet through the gravel, praying he'll give me a lift, at least to Kearney. Later on I'll think of something good to say, some perfect comeback topped with whipped cream and a smile.

"Well, don't just stand there, git in if you wanna."

He unhitches the lock and stares at me through the window, like he's daring me.

I have never turned down a dare in my life and I'm not about to start now, just cause I can't think of nothing clever to say to turn me into the starlet of his private movie. I put my head back on my shoulders, real high, open the door and hop in. There is a moment of silence while we both contemplate our new situation.

"You got any money?" He doesn't look at me when he says it. He looks straight ahead, calculating into the sun.

"No, but I'm good at stealing."

"Well, at least you're good for something."

Then he peels off onto the road so fast the back of the truck swishes out over the gravel in a C and something in my heart lurches forward, like a roller coaster at the very top, when you can't see what's coming but you're bracing for a steep drop.

SIX

He stays stone quiet all the way to the panhandle and I find this to be just a little bit aggravating. Whenever a guy around me isn't talking I always assume he's thinking of all the reasons why he doesn't like me and all the ways he's gonna get rid of me. Not that I like this particular aspect of my personality. It's weak and helpless and where I see my mama in myself. Tammy can't stand it if there's even one single nothing of a man slunking somewhere in the corner of the room not paying her no mind. Just that little itty-bitty portion of neglect drives her nutso. And I'll be honest, some of that suction-cup need to be looked at and keened over and adored has been inherited by yours truly. I make a pact now, this very moment, telling myself to change it. Right here and now.

Next time I will just imagine that whenever any boy or guy or Marlboro man is silent around me, it's because he's just so deep in thought about how hard he has fallen in love with me and that look of furrowed exasperation on his brow is only a reaction to his feeling of utter helplessness. This will be my new factory for turning lemons into lemonade. Sometimes if you can trick yourself into thinking something, really trick yourself so you don't even know what's true anymore, you can make that something come true. I resolve to break hearts.

My companion doesn't know it, but I have been inspecting him for the last fifteen minutes and I have noticed a few things that differentiate him from the regular shitbag you see on the street.

Number one, he's crooked.

Now, when I say crooked, I don't mean it in any sort of poetic sense. I mean he's crooked. Literally. Like his body looks like an italic. He veers to the left, like he's crippled or bent or swayed off to the side.

Number two, his brow overhangs the rest of his face like a cliff. It's like there's a candy bar buried somewhere underneath the skin above his eyes, giving him a troubled look of constant consternation. .

Number three, when he wrinkles his forehead, it makes a V-shape instead of a regular line, like most people, adding to his look of infinite struggle.

Number four, his legs are longer and skinnier than anything you've ever seen attached to a body. He's like some kind of daddy-long-legs spindling behind the wheel.

Number five, his eyes look like they're about to pop right out of his head. They seem bigger than the average eyes and less attached to their respective sockets. They oogle around like toy button eyes on a sock puppet.

Now, I know this list does not sound very flattering. I know that. But there is something about him, some thing in the air around him, that makes me want him to fall out of his seat in love with me. There is nothing logical about it. It's something about the ions buzzing around his head that makes me want him to grab me and pull me over and reach down between my legs.

I look over at him and assess his feelings. Not interested. In his oogly eyes, I'm just a kid, some kind of little girl you might pat on the head at the ball game before putting your arm around your real girlfriend and walking off under the bleachers. I scrutinize him, watching while he stares straight ahead, gripping the wheel with that candy bar buried beneath his brow bone. I decide he is all bark and no bite.

"So . . . do you have a girlfriend?"

"No." He stays looking at the road, like I'm some speck of dust not worth it.

"Why . . . don't you like girls?"

(I know how to rile them up.)

"Depends."

None too successful.

"Wull . . . what kinda girls you like?"

"Quiet ones."

Okay, now I'm really losing my touch. This requires something drastic.

"Um . . . do you mind not looking over here for a while?"

"What for?"

"I kinda been wearing the same thing all day and I'd like to change."

"Knock yourself out, kid."

I wait a second to let it sink in, this impending nakedness. I'm gonna make his eyes swirl if it kills me. I struggle to take off my T-shirt, like it's somehow impossible and caught, to give him time to think about what I'm doing and just what's going on over on this side of the truck. Then I pull my dress on over my head and down around my American thighs. Every once in a while I steal a quick glance at my companion, to see if he's hooked.

He's staring at the road ahead real intent, gripping the wheel, composed and forceful. He doesn't look over but I can tell I'm starting to wiggle under his skin. And now, for the grand finale. I take off my jeans and don't even have to pretend to struggle with this one because taking off jeans in a beat-up pick-up truck going eighty miles an hour on a rolling gravel road in the pitch black is no cakewalk. Finally I just kick them off, quick, and pull down my skirt. There's a moment of nothing much and then my companion looks me over, beginning to see the potential for the speck of dust beside him to turn from cubic zirconia to white diamonds.

"That doesn't match."

"What do you mean?"

"Cowboy boots and that dress. That doesn't match. Unless you're a hooker."

He laughs at himself, thinking he's Mr. Wit and oh so old and wise.

"Oh, so now I'm a hooker?"

"Look, darlin, you're too ripe is the problem."

"Excuse me?"

"I said you're too ripe. And your mouth's too big. You got a big mouth."

"What do you mean I got a big mouth? You mean like it's too big, in general, or like I talk too much?"

"Both."

"Wull, what do I care anyways."

"What was that?"

"What do you know anyways, you're nothing but a fucking cripple."

He stops the truck so fast my head slams forward about an inch off the dashboard and I wonder if my nervous hospital judgment wasn't so far off base. I sit dumb trying to wonder how I can switch things back from minor to major. This is the part where I'm scared, but there's something in my fear, something else, like I want him to get mad and fly off the handle and show me what he's got.

"You listen to me, you little brat, if you ever, ever say that again, I'll throw you straight through this windshield and run you over after that. Understood?"

We stare at each other, double-dare.

"Let me out."

"What? Speak up. I can't hear you?"

"Let me out."

"Door's right there. Feel free to use it."

"Okay. I will and fuck you, you fucking gimp."

And with that he lunges over me, opens the door and pushes me and all my worldly belongings out in one fell swoop. I land on the ground in the dirt and he peels off before I can say I'm fine. Before I dust myself off or stand up and show him I'm capable of walking on my own, he's over the next hill and into the night.

Well, that's that, I guess.

I look into the night sky, pitch black with stars so bright you wonder why you can't just hop on one and ride away. The corn smells sweet behind me, heading off row by row into the pitch black. There are no cars. No lights for miles. Not even a telephone pole to give you comfort.

I walk myself gently into the ditch. Whenever I feel like this, I am gentle with myself, pretend like I'm someone else, someone good. I walk on eggshells around myself, like I'm some fragile piece of porcelain you have to place quietly, deliberately back on the shelf.

I put my jeans and T-shirt on the ground to make a bed, then set my bag up top for the pillow. Home sweet home. My first night out was not a stunning success. Maybe I was too thirsty for my new life. I lay my head back on my makeshift pillow and decide that tomorrow I will behave in a manner that is slow. Tomorrow I will let things happen to me, instead of trying to make things happen. Tomorrow I will try to be softer.

SEVEN

They could sure make these ditches more comfortable. Maybe hold back on the brambles part. I'm tossing and turning and all I can think is how you're not supposed to be an all-alone girl, especially at night. If you're an all-alone girl at night, might as well call it quits.

I keep thinking about this all-alone lady we got for a schoolteacher. She had a look like she was raised in the basement of a library. She had mousy-brown bangs and sun-scared skin the color of paper. She came here from some college back East with no men and that's the way they want it. She got invited to two barbecues, one bake-off, and that was that cause she liked to get mad about what kind of beer you drank or don't say sweetie, say Miss Crisp.

It wasn't long after she got transferred that she started staring at me round the clock. I went from back left to center center to front right, like tic-tac-toe, in five days straight. She put me right up front and this is what she'd do. She'd take a long, leisurely stroll round the room and stop, oh so casual, right smack-bang behind yours truly. She'd put her eyes in my socks, in my shoes, in my hair and just stay planted there till test over. I swear to Betsy she made those tests up, pop quiz, just to take a peek. And I kept trying to hate her. I did, but then came the day she caught me red-handed.

She caught me red-handed cause there was this girl in my class, three rows up, who spent all recess mirror in hand. Kids would be running round like it was the end of the world and four- square and dodge-ball and there she'd be, smack-dab in the middle, statue still, staring in that silver vanity mirror you're supposed to keep in a drawer.

I don't care about that. Who'd care about that part? She could've stared at that mirror till her head popped off and fine with me. That's not the point. The point is she wouldn't eat her sandwich. That's the point.

The point is she'd eat the apple, the pudding cup, the crackers and toss the sandwich, the whole sandwich, back in the bag and then in the trash and forget it. The point is that sandwich would get left back, all alone, and I'd feel sorry for it. I felt sorry for that sand-wich, and so one day I took it upon myself to do something about it. The point is her mom sure knew how to make a sandwich.

Okay, I'll admit it. Miss Crisp caught me, hands in the trash-can, trying to make that sandwich feel a little less lonely. She caught me and she didn't send me to the principal or tell my folks or noth-ing. Instead, she invited me over for Friday dinner, nothing special, in case I didn't have plans. It wasn't a holiday, just Friday dinner, don't get worked up about it.

Or so I thought.

But then, guess what, I show up Friday and it's like Jesus, Mary and Joseph are expected at eight. She's got mashed potatoes and salad with Dorothy Lynch and Jell-O with marshmallows in it. She's got rump roast with gravy and two different pies, pecan or pumpkin, you take your pick. She's got bread in a loaf, no slices, and olive oil and mashed-up tomatoes with pepper, spread it on the bread. She's got stuff I've never seen, don't even know how to eat, let alone when, there's not enough time.

And maybe something about the look on my face or the shoveling of rump roast or the quickness of courses and asking for seconds, maybe something about the two pieces of pie and wanting three, maybe something about the quiet around the table when I look up and see the schoolteacher staring down, furrowing a line between her brow, makes for a knock on my front door the next day.

That little schoolteacher with paper skin comes walking over, through the weeds and up our rickety steps, framing herself in the front door, with a worried look on her forehead and a bag of Tupperware weighing down her spindly pencil arm.

It was not the best time to make a house-call.

In fact, maybe just never make a house-call next time.

This is what happened. There was the little problem of Tammy being out all night the night before, no explanation, no nothing, just not back at noon the next day and mind your own business, don't ask questions. That was the first part.

The second part was that, as the hours dragged by from night into late night into early morning into the next goddamn day and still nothing cocksucker, my dad went from having a shot of Jack to pass the time to having a shot of Jack to take the edge off to having a shot to calm his nerves and then another to calm the fuck down and Jesus Christ where the fuck is my wife and where the fuck is your goddamn mother and then the bottle gets empty and then the bottle gets thrown and the dad is sitting on the stairs with his head in his hands sobbing. Sobbing.

And that's when the knock comes.

It's not the police with a sad, tragic but earnest report about the whereabouts of my mama. It's not Uncle Nipper and Aunt Gina stumbling in with Tammy in tow, talking about it was a rough night and you should have been there you'd never believe it. In fact, it's got nothing to do with Tammy at all.

It is, instead, a paper-thin spindle of a thing with skin the color of glue, standing squint-eyed in the doorway.

My dad peeks through the side window, jolts and cleans up his act, throwing back his shoulders and taking his place with a casual cowboy lean before opening the door. You better just prepare yourself to answer doors in my house.

She stands there, the schoolteacher, she stands there, looking up at him, big and gruff and mean and tall and leaning in like the Marlboro man. She stands there, stammering, looking up at him, up all night and smelling of whiskey and looking like he's itching for a fight, just give him a reason. She stands there, the schoolteacher, no bigger than a thimble, in her scuffed-up Buster Brown shoes.

"Um. Hello. Um. My name is Miss Crisp. I teach at Luli's school and, well, we had dinner the other night, last night, We had a wonderful time, really, and so, well, I thought I'd bring Luli some leftovers, just in case she—"

And then he kisses her.

That's right. My dad grabs Miss Crisp by the waist, pulls her off her feet and kisses her on the mouth for ten seconds straight, with her legs dangling from his forearm.

The bag of Tupperware falls to the floor, forget about the Tupperware, no one's thinking about that now. Now it's just my dad whisking the little brown-haired wisp of a schoolteacher off her feet when she went to a school with no vowels and no men, that's for damn sure, that's the way they want it.

Now it's just him setting her back down on the ground, easy, still looking into her eyes, her backing up, stunned, flummoxed, dizzy. Now it's just her composing herself, smoothing down her sweater, backing up, backing up, flustered and blushing, turning around, stymied, making her way, barely, down the steps, through the weeds and back home.

Now it's just him looking after her, my dad, looking after her, smiling to himself and shaking his head, following her with his eyes all the way down the steps and up the dirt road. He laughs out loud, my dad, making his way backwards up the stairs into the bedroom. He chuckles to himself, over and over, my dad, before falling into bed with his clothes on, snickering himself to sleep and throwing back the night.

I grab the Tupperware and thank God and all twelve apostles for the marshmallow Jell-O, mashed potatoes and fancy bread with no slices. I say a prayer that this'll mark a brand new phase of my life, of my dad and Miss Crisp and rump roast with carrots or peas, you take your pick.

I make a promise to the ceiling and the upstairs beyond that I will do whatever it takes, be good and never swear, if this could be my new day dawning, with corn on the cob and pumpkin pie and my dad laughing silly up the stairs. I won't lie or cheat or swear or steal, I promise.

But the schoolteacher never comes back. She never comes back and never says another word about two kinds of pie or rump roast or kisses on the porch that sweep you off your feet.

But she does one nice thing that I'll never talk back to. From that day on, every morning, when I look in my desk, there it is. It's a tiny little brown paper bag and inside is grapes and a grainy kind of food, God knows what, and not one but two, two Fred Flintstone vitamins for dessert. That's the candy part.

And I don't know if it's the way my daddy swept her off her feet or the way I can't seem to get an F, but that little schoolteacher, with skin the color of paper, takes me back from being the full bad person I'm meant to be. She puts a light on in the attic and keeps it on, just barely.

But, boy, you should've seen her blush. That paper turned red all right.

Once I get to Vegas I'm gonna find someone to make my legs dangle.

EIGHT

Sometime deep into the night I am awakened from my grassy slumber by the sound of something streaming steadily beside me, up a ways in the ditch. I sit up and squint blindly into the dark. Much to my surprise or fear or wondering if it's just a late night vision, I see a woman there, standing upright in the moonlight. Her skirt is jacked up above her hips and her legs spread, pissing straight down like a man, miraculous in her accuracy. Her high heels are dug into the dirt and she seems, at that moment, to be some kind of superhero, able to leap tall buildings in a single bound, or at least to stand straight upright and piss boy-style.

She's pretty, not so much from some glossy, made-up, magazine-like imitation but in that way that has something to do with knowing or feeling or having been up to no good. Like trouble. She has that same blond Doris Day flip like my mama, only with a little more roots and a lot more hairspray. She doesn't see me. She just stands there pissing casual over the night.

I watch her with a weird little thrill that she doesn't see me but I see her, till I remember my predicament and have a vision of her driving away, leaving me behind, without a trace. And that would not do.

"Jesus, lady, you trying to piss on my head?"

She starts, not exactly a jump, but I know I surprised her, which seems not easy to do, judging from the look on her face when she spots me in the dirt. She sighs through her lips, almost like a pout and a sigh met on the dance floor and went for a whirl.

"Holy fucker, kid, you could give someone a heart attack yelping out from the ditch like that."

"That was not a yelp, and anyways, you bout pissed on my head."

"Sorry, I didn't see ya." She susses me out. "What the hell ya doing out here anyways? You oughta be in bed."

"I am in bed."

"You some kinda runaway or something?"

She takes a cigarette out of her purse and lights it, throwing the match down and squishing it into the ground with the front of her heel. I take note that, within her peeing extravaganza, she didn't seem to bother with any kind of panties.

"How can you pee standing up like that?"

"Whattaya mean?"

"I mean, don't you have to squat a little? I always have to squat a little."

"Naw. Not if you're smart. You just find where the hill goes down, move your feet out the way and shoot."

After that, we just sort of stare at each other. There's something about her I like. Something familiar, like she's just leaning through this life and not caring too much about the walls falling down around her. She doesn't seem like the kind of person that would tell you to sit up straight or wash your mouth out with soap or scold you for elbows on the table. She looks like what I want to look like.

"So, you gonna tell me why you're out here or are you trying to be mysterious?"

"I got in a fight."

"Oh." She nods. "Boyfriend?"

"Naw. Just some guy picked me up on the side of the road. He seemed all right but then he kind of got crazy and I just looked at him and said, 'Let me out,' and he tried to make me stay, begged me actually, but finally I just opened the door and got out."

"Well. Good for you. That's smart." She takes a drag. "You're smart. That's the kinda thing happens all the time. Think someone's okay and then they start to act real nutso and turn into some snoring shitbag and next thing you know you're tied to the bathtub."

I stare at her, in awe, like she's some highway angel sent down from heaven to school me in the ways of shitbags and nutsos and snoring in the dark.

She shakes her head, private, taking the last drag off her cigarette. She drops the cherry into the ground and snuffs it out by windshield wiping the front of her heel. She doesn't seem to remember I'm still there.

She sighs and looks back at her car. It's a bright white LeBaron and propped up in the passenger seat is a giant, stuffed, yellow-and-white bunny rabbit. It's just sitting there, looking out like it's waiting for the burger girl to roller-skate over and hand over a tray of fries. It's a human-size bunny rabbit with big black button eyes and a broken-off piece of thread where the nose is supposed to be. It must be at least six feet tall and there's something kind of sinister about it. You get the feeling it's just itching to hurl itself over to the driver's side and drive right off.

I look back over to my newfound angel, hoping for an explanation, but she's half-way back to the car by now. Soon as she gets to the driver's side, she opens the door and says, "Well, kid. Good luck. Stay straight. See ya around."

She gets in and starts the engine.

Well, this is not how I imagined it. What sort of lady would just drive off into the night leaving some kid face down in the dirt? Her sort, I guess.

"Hey, lady . . . wait up!"

I get up fast as I can and run up to the driver's side window, cracked open. She just sits there, dome light on, putting on lipstick in the rearview mirror like she's got a date with the road. The bunny stares straight ahead, plotting into the windshield through his black button eyes.

"Look, lady, I know you don't know me and a pretty lady like you probably never does a favor for anyone, probably never has to, what with having the world on a string and whatnot . . ."

She looks up from her lipstick.

"Whattaya want, kid?"

"Umm . . . wull . . . I wanna come with you, I guess. I want a ride."

"Well, as you can see, I've got company." She gestures towards the bunny, taking out her compact and powdering her nose. The bunny stands his ground.

"Please."

I make a face like the last dog left at the pound. I feel about two feet tall but I am not about to spend the rest of the night in the brambles.

"Hmph." She looks me up and down, weighing the pros and cons of having a tagalong. "Where you headed?"

"Las Vegas."

She clicks her compact closed and looks at me.

"Well, what a coincidence, so am I."

She smiles and all the sudden there's this glow around her, like a halo or a hidden lamp, like she could block out the moon.

"Get in. But just to warn you, I ain't giving any handouts."

"That's okay. I got my own . . . just a sec." I run back to collect my worldly belongings, yelling over the motor, "I got plenty of money, so don't worry, that's the last thing you gotta worry about." I look at the bunny rabbit in the passenger seat, waiting for some kind of cue. She stretches out back, unlatching the back-door lock. I throw my bag in and sit down proud, like I'm expecting her to throw me a bone.

"Look, kid, lesson number one."

I slam the door.

"You can't go around telling people stuff like that."

"Like what?"

"Like about money, and having plenty of it. That just marks you right there, understand?"

"Yeah."

"Good. Don't forget it. Hey, you like Patsy Cline?"

"Who?"

"Patsy Cline? Heard of her? Yes? No? Well, whatever, you better learn to like her cause that's all you're gonna be hearing from here to Las Vegas."

"Great."

"I'll teach you the words if you want. You can croon along. Won't mean nothing to you, though. Nothing means nothing until you get your heart broke."

We glide away into the night, leaving my little home away from home to the crickets and the ants. I lean back and listen to some song about seven lonely days making one lonely week. I press my head sideways against the window, looking up at the black sky and the bunny ears in front of me, wondering what and who will break my heart.

NINE

So, what's your name, kid?" She says it out the corner of her mouth, lighting a cigarette, squinting down at the car lighter.

"Luli."

"Luli?" She eyes me sideways, figuring I'm making it up.

"Yup."

"What kind of a name is that?"

"I don't know."

I feel shy next to her prettiness. She's got that look like there's a spotlight framing her, backing her up and keeping the evil spirits at bay. Like in those black-and-white movies when the soldier wakes up in the hospital after fighting the Germans and there all the sudden is this white-dressed dreamboat turning the world from dirt to ice cream with a flip of her hair. I wouldn't call her cute. And not beautiful, either. Just pretty. Real pretty. Easy on the eyes.

"Well, I'll tell you what kind of name it is. Strange. It's a strange name." She ashes out the window. "And I'd be willing to bet you're a strange kid. Strange name, strange kid. It follows. Not your fault. No fault of yours. Just stands to reason that that's what ends up happening. That's why you gotta be careful. There's this couple in Memphis that named their kid Mickey Mouse. Mickey Mouse. Can you believe it? They had ten kids, so the last one, they just threw up their hands and said, 'Okay, Mickey Mouse. That's your name. Good luck.'"

"Wull, what's your name?"

"Glenda."

There's a moment of silence cause I can't think of nothing smart.

"You from around here?" She lets me off the hook.

"Yup . . . um, Palmyra. Maybe you know my dad. Nicholas Scott McMullen."

"People call him Nick?"

"Yeah, you know him?" I say, all hope and glory. I sound like a small town girl. Small potatoes.

"Nope."

"Oh."

"I just figured . . ."

"Oh, right." I laugh a little, embarrassed. I can see her eyes in the rearview. She smiles, not wanting to be mean. That's where that light comes from. It's like she comes from a place where you can just sit there and don't have to cut down.

"Okay." She nods, "Well, now that we've got that established, what about your mother?"

"What about her?"

She sizes me up in the mirror. "What's the matter, you got some pending issue or something?"

I don't say nothing.

"All right." She tosses her cigarette out the window. "They know you're out here?"

"No."

"Bet they're worried."

"I doubt it. My dad left and my mama's fucking a peeled worm."

She laughs at that, a hearty laugh, like she's on the Tonight Show.

So, how'd you get stuck out in the ditch like that? You're about three hours west of Palmyra."

"I hitched a ride from some guy. He was crazy."

"They all are. Some're just better at hiding it."

I stare out the window at the pitch black, the only light coming out from the headlights, endless and straight.

"Well, what'd he look like?"

"Who?"

"The guy."

"Crazy. Bug-eyed. A real freak."

Her ears start to prick up.

"Whattaya mean, bug-eyed?"

"You know, bug-eyed. Like a frog, kinda."

She gets real quiet now. I can feel something sizzling in the molecules circling around her.

"You get his name?"

"Eddie. Eddie Kreezer."

"Tell me you did not just say that."

"I did not just say that . . . but that was his name. Eddie Kreezer."

"Good motherfucking Lord almighty." She slams her hands on the dashboard. "Jesus."

All the sudden everything's changed and that light around her turns from white to red.

I shuffle my feet, look at my shoes, not knowing what to say or do or what to make of it. Finally I say the dumbest thing ever.

"Know him?"

"Know him?" She laughs, but it's an unhappy laugh. "Yeah, I guess I do know him. I know him better than he knows himself."

"What?"

"Nothing. Goddamnit . . . good thing you got outta that car."

"Truck."

"What?"

"He was driving a truck."

"Oh, I see, he drives a truck now. Well, that's perfect. Probably crashed that old Buick. Good Lord." She sighs. "Boy, he is just one bad apple. Just rotten to the core."

She grabs another cigarette off the dash, where each cigarette is lined up, one by one, in a row, a ready-to-smoke system conceived of in some brilliant moment of necessity into invention.

"So . . . did ya think he's cute?" She clicks in the cigarette lighter.

"No. Wull. I don't know."

"Yeah, there's something about him, I know. Even though he's so ugly. There is something. Hell, he had me fooled."

She lights her cigarette.

"One thing about him, though. He was just real weird, you know, like he had a few screws loose or something. Whatever, I probably shouldn't be tellin you this, anyways. Did he call you darlin?"

"Yup."

We drive on silent, the road disappearing underneath us into the dark.

"Okay, here's the plan. If we stop anywhere, and I do mean any-where, and there he is . . . run, don't walk, back to the car, lock the door and duck. No questions. No talking. We'll just take off. Got it? Lesson two. Although, that's more like a rule. We'll call it rule slash lesson two."

She takes a drag off her cigarette. I shuffle in my seat. I've been nodding at her this whole time, pretending like I'm right there with her, more so than the bunny rabbit.

"Guys like that, you just gotta put to bed. Kiss them good night. Turn out the light. Walk out the door. Cut your losses."

She goes to put her cigarette out in the ashtray and I can see her hands are shaking. I want to change the subject but I don't know how to without making her feel like she's just been spilling her guts out while I've been counting fence-posts. She starts reaching be-hind her, grabbing around the backseat, steering this way and that, not paying no mind to the zig-zag we're making on the asphalt. It's starting to get reckless and maybe just a bit too carefree for comfort.

"Um, you want me to help, while you steer?"

"Yeah, kid, sure, can you hand me my purse? It's red."

I nod, relieved, and search the backseat beside me, through the puzzle of wrinkled clothes and empty cigarette cartons, wanting to make her like me. I pull out a ruby-colored alligator rectangle with a gold clasp. She sure has good taste. Classy.

"All right, now, you hand that to me and reach up over here and grab the wheel."

I do what she says, leaning awkward over the seat. She unclasps the gold and pulls out a tiny oriental vial with a dragon on it, squiggling up the side. She presses it to her nose and sniffs up hard, tilting her head back. Her face freezes for a second, like the world is on hold. I am watching her with every bone in my body, trying not to drive us into the ditch. I feel like I'm with a movie star.

And then I remember something, something about the sniffing back hard and the back-of-the-knuckles wiping off the nose. I know it. I know it cause my dad got fired from the Kuhnel farm down on Highway 34 and there was five days of sniffing back and knuckle cleaning and white powder and never sleeping and some guy named Randy that I'd never seen before and never saw since.

There it was, for all the world to see, cut out in lines on the kitchen table and a dollar bill rolled up and razor scraping, always scraping, for just a little bit left. And there was my dad and Randy, the new-best-friend stranger, with all their plans of all this stuff they were gonna do, like start an alpaca farm or make a ranch out of tires or open up a barbecue slash strip joint down on Savage Boulevard.

And he would get up, my dad would, and start pacing around the floor and gesticulating all around the room and they were gonna get this guy to do this and they knew that that guy would do that other thing for free and they were gonna have the whole world on a string, no doubt about it, right after doing this next line.

And there was no sleeping or eating or even going out. It was just days and days of this new ingenious scheme and that new old contact to make and they were gonna have just about every cousin and high school buddy and long lost lover on the payroll and it was gonna be a golden day until sometime in the middle of day five when Tammy came walking up the driveway back from visiting Aunt Gina in Alliance. And I was sure glad to see her cause by this point I was getting down to the last dregs of the leftover Halloween candy, and a girl just can't live on lollipops the way she can live off Snickers, and I am just hoping Tammy doesn't wring my neck for letting this go on so long.

She walks through the front door and takes one look at the lines going up the table and the new-best-friend stranger and the hole someone made in the ceiling somewhere in the middle of day two, and I swear to God you could have taken that razor right off the table and cut little lines up into the air cause there ain't nothing or no one could freeze your blood cold inside your body like my mama.

Dad tries to make it better by giving a little half laugh and introducing Randy, saying, "He's a great guy, you oughta get to know him."

And that's it.

She doesn't even say nothin. That's how bad it is. She just marches straight across the room, grabs my hand and walks out the front door and takes off, me by her side, for three weeks back with Aunt Gina in Alliance. When we come back there's no sign of Randy or the lines on the table and even the hole in the ceiling is patched up with white and painted over in blotches.

No, there was no physical sign, no evidence of the preceding events. There was nothing you could point to and say, "A-ha! That was it. That's what did it." There was nothing tangible that might have helped you put together in your head that now things were different. That, when before my mama used to come over with honey words and hair scruffing in those times of woe when my dad used to bow his head down and wonder how he was gonna turn the world into an oyster for me and my mama, that now . . . that now there were no more silk spun words and cotton-candy assurances. Now there was just silent resentment. Now there was just disappointment that he'd never amount to nothing. Now there was just looming hatred and wishing she could be someplace else and the crushing realization that she'd made a mistake.

And that's not all. Now there was going out late and looking for something else. Someone else. Now there was late night giggling and coming home and pretending she wasn't screwing around with you-know-who from down at the factory. Now there was just the constant piddling escape from endless days of defeat with a flirt here and a dash out the back there and anything, just anything, to make it better, please make it better, even for just fifteen minutes in the dark behind the Alibi.

"Okay, kid, you game?"

Glenda wakes me from my musing and I'm glad to be back. I do not want to spend my days dreaming with my eyes getting wetter and my jaw getting tight. That was that time, behind me, never again. Never again. I'll flip the switch on it, and it'll be off and off for good. Flip.

Glenda grabs the wheel back and hands the vial over. She senses my hesitation. She doesn't know the half of it and I am not about to tell her. I slink back, staring at that swirling dragon, red and better not.

"Okay, look, how old are you?"

"Thirteen"

"Thirteen, huh?" She thinks. "Well, sooner or later, you're gonna be doing this. At least trying it. And it's probably gonna be with some fat slob that just wants to get in your pants. So, I figure, you might as well try it in a safe environment with someone that ain't after nothing X-rated. See what I mean?"

She looks at me and gives a shrug like who cares anyways. I think about it, forgetting about all the bad stuff from my previous life, which no longer exists because I flipped the switch. I decide she has a point. My previous life no longer exists, no way, no how. I should just do what I would have done without knowing anything about it.

I take the vial, put it up to my nose and sniff at it like she did. Nothing much.

"You gotta snort harder, cover your other nostril and sniff it up fast."

I do it like she says and it's like someone just burnt a hole through my nose and back into my eyes. It feels like pins and needles, numbing me from inside my face. I sit back and wait to start seeing things. She reaches back for the vial, takes it from me and puts it between her legs, out of sight. We're both sniffing to ourselves, not talking, just sitting there, rubbing our noses, electrified. She reaches for a cigarette and offers me one. I'm like her now. I'm a big girl. I can take it. I roll down the window and light my cigarette off hers, leaning forward. I have this feeling, this amped-up feeling like I'm better than I am, like we're movie stars and this is the part where you're meeting us for the first time and wondering who we are and what danger lies before us.

Outside, all there is rolling past us is two giant orange trucks, scooping out the side of a hill and one man with a bullhorn, yelling orders.

"When do I start, um, seeing things?"

"Seeing things?"

"You know, hallucinating, like, seeing stuff . . ."

She laughs out loud but doesn't look back at me. Her eyes in the rearview, serious and mean. She keeps scrunching her mouth together and licking her lips. She has that look in her eyes like my uncle used to get when someone from out of town came into the bar, like she's chomping at the bit to start a scrap.

"Well, kid, there ain't no seeing stuff goes along with this. That's not what this is, see. This is not one of those things that takes you out of everything. No sir. This is something that puts you right back in."

I nod, meaningful, pretending I know exactly what she's getting at. I feel fast, now, anxious. We're going about 100 miles an hour but it feels like 900 and I feel like any second now we're going to cata-pult off the ground and fly straight into the stars.

"Um, Glenda, do you ever go to church?"

"Nope. Lookit, kid, God doesn't go to church . . . he goes on first dates and stuff."

"Well, you ever seen him?"

"Not at church, that's for damn sure."

"Well, have you ever seen him on a first date?"

"Lookit, kid, stay focused, we're gonna need to stay awake if we're gonna make it in time."

"In time for what?"

This is the first I heard of any time constraint, schedule, or anything to do with the outside world, the world outside this car, the world outside this movie with this woman and this girl and this bunny rabbit.

I don't like it.

"Oh, I'll tell you later, it's kind of a long story. You know, I've got some things you might be interested in. Little things. Along the way. Things you could do for me or with me or we could do together, helpful things. I mean, you never know, this could turn out to be a real blessing."

She turns back and looks me over, up and down.

"Are you wily, kid?"

"What do you mean?"

"Are you wily, you know, street smart, like, if a ship sank and you were on it, you know you'd be the one waiting, floating on some piece of bark when the rescue boat came, sharks circling around you, sunburned. That kinda thing."

"Yeah. Yeah. I guess I am. I don't wanna toot my own horn, but I do believe I am."

"Yup, that's what I thought. You seem like it. Seem like there's something kinda mean up in there. Seem like you'd catch on quick."

The sun is coming up behind us. I can just start to make out the rows upon rows of corn streaming up along beside us. At this speed they look like a jagged leafy fence, smudged, blowing by.

"Why do you keep that bunny rabbit in the front seat?" I just ask it, might as well get it over with.

She doesn't hear me, or maybe she does and chooses to ignore it.

"You know one thing about a man, if you ever find one that you like, is, he's gotta know how to fuck you. Rich. Poor. Cute. It don't matter. He's gotta know how to lay you down on your back, spread your legs and fuck you."

I stare at the corn.

"I know, I know, maybe I shouldn't talk like that in front of you. But it's good you learn it now. Lotta girls just go with any old boring suit or some fatso with a job sending her flowers, then they wonder why they're so miserable and why they get so ugly and sad and old. They say to themselves, staring at the ceiling, husband snoring away beside them, 'What the hell happened? Where'd all the time go? When did I get so old and sad and wrinkly?' I'll tell you when, when you were lying underneath that fat shitbag who couldn't fuck a woman if he had a step-by-step guide. And they never say, 'This is not enough. Laying here, yawning, while this fat fuck pokes at me until he rolls over and starts snoring.' Because if you don't say that, listen to me, here, if you don't say that, they'll reel you in. They'll play nice and buy flowers and reel you into their pathetic little life and the next thing you know, you don't even remember your own name. It's just Mrs. Something-or-Other. Mrs. Shitbag. See what I mean? No way. Not me. Not fucking me."

"Wull, um, do you even like guys?"

"Phumph." I feel like I said something stupid but then she smiles to herself. "I like em when I first meet em. When they're putting on the Ritz. But, you know, it's all downhill from there."

She takes the vial from between her thighs, opens it up and snorts again. She's starting to lose that halo around her. In the morning light, she's not all glamour. She's starting to look a little less heaven-sent and a little more like someone you might see down at the track. In the mirror, I see now about how she has tiny wrinkles threatening to spread across her forehead. I'm watching her and I'm thinking to myself that I can't tell if she's good or bad. She's one of those people you don't know about until something happens, something big. And I'm wondering, as I look at her wheat-spun hair in the golden light, what, exactly, that something will be.

TEN

Now, I am not a lesbo, and I do not intend on signing up, but it just so happens that when I look at Glenda, when I listen to Glenda, I get this feeling in my gut like I want to jump inside her, like the space between me and her is too great, too distant, and if I could just smash up against her maybe I could see the world through her eyes.

She catches me looking at her.

"Do you know where we're going, kid?"

"Nope."

Nothing I say comes out natural because I'm too busy trying to sound natural.

The sun is straight up in the sky now, blazing down in a line, boring a hole through the top of the roof. The bunny rabbit sits listless in the front, tired of this new back-seat tag-along. The flatlands spread out in beige and green square patches sprawled out into the horizon for miles and nothing there. None too colorful, not like the McDonald's commercials where the sun comes up against a farmhouse and someone's rooster starts to cock-a-doodle-doo into the golden light, ringing in the arrival of hash browns and sausage. Not here, this is mostly shades of drab and drabber, stretching out to eternity and no promise in it.

I saw pictures of the East Coast in school. It was green and everything was scrunched up together, like they had no idea everyone was coming, so they just make-shift stuck everything together and hoped it'd work out. And I read that sixty-two percent of everybody in America is just sitting there between Boston and Washington, D.C., waiting for something to happen, piled on top of each other, like a beehive, this box inside that box inside that box.

The East Coast is where you get to go when you're out of school, if you're from Lincoln and a member of the Knolls Country Club and live on Sheridan. You get to come back all chuffed up on Thanksgiving and make a circle with all the other older brother Chads and cousin Jennys about this game and that class and how you had to stay up till five last week just to get three papers done and then about fell asleep in class and ha ha ha you sure felt silly.

And you could be like me and sit there dripping in your towel at the Knolls, like some wet rat, out of place, invited on a lark, practically by mistake, out of politeness to Becky's cousin Cindy, but ending up there regardless and listening. And you might think to yourself, What kind of world is this that lies somewhere outside the drip-drab horizon with rolling hills and halls of granite, green and books? What kind of world is this that nobody told me about that extends its hands out to nowheresville and plucks lovingly, exclusively, the cream of the crop? Who the hell gets to go there and why and if it's Cindy then she ain't near smart enough and why her not me?

You might think that. And it might tear you up for a second and make you run inside the locker room before anyone catches on that that's not just swimming-pool water running down your face and before everybody starts whispering, Who the hell invited that girl? Well, you might as well just hold up a sign that says, "I don't belong here just take me back to shitsville."

But if you're smart, you'll just bite down and forget you ever heard it. Just pretend that was some black-and-white movie and that whole snooty universe doesn't exist or it might as well not cause it sure as hell doesn't exist for you.

And never will.

You don't want to be squeezed in between sixty-two percent of snootsville, anyways. Bunch of limp city folk that couldn't figure out how to pour whiskey out of a boot with directions on the heel.

I stare out at the fields in green and yellow patches rolling by into the dusk coming up from behind. Glenda sits in the front, knuckles turning white on the wheel, shoulders hunched and leaning forward, heading west.

Out west everything has its own space. Every little ramshackle cabin, shack, hut sits perched atop its own little piece of destiny with room to breathe, room to live, room to die. You'll see them, the dead ones, sitting by the side of the road like some faded gray and rotting mystery, thinking about the good ol days before trains and cars and wanting more.

And you'd best be prepared for heading west. Otherwise, you might just end up eating your best friend's ankle, hunkered up under a snowdrift somewhere, like the Donners . . . marking the bodies so you don't eat your own uncle, watching your pastor starve to death, calculating his weight versus the rest of winter. And you might look over at that one nutso German and have the sneaking suspicion he's just killing people and eating them before they die, on a whim, for fun.

But that was out by Reno. Here, before Chimney Rock, it wasn't quite that dramatic. Mostly, in the panhandle, folks just froze to death, uneventful. You'd be wandering around after your dream and you'd come across some half-thawed Swede in the slush. And you'd look at him, shrug your shoulders and say a prayer, but you weren't about to stop.

I look out past the corn and the wheat and wonder how many sets of bones are buried, unspoken, keeping their stories to themselves in the dirt. I wonder if they know the sky is bright blue today and the air smells sweet. I wonder if they still listen in. I wonder if the caterpillar trucks will roll over them, too.

Glenda pipes up from the front seat.

"Okay, kid, here's how it's gonna be. And no naysaying. If you naysay even once, I'm gonna kick that door open and throw you out after. I mean it. Nobody likes a naysayer. Nobody, got it? So, we gotta get to Jackson. Never mind why. Just that we're headed to Jackson for some very specific reasons that I'll tell you later. On the way, we're gonna have to make a few stops, see, for provisions. Now, on these stops, you're gonna have to do a little acting. You ever acted before?"

"Only my whole life."

"Okay, good. That's good. Now, did you ever see, on TV or in the movies or something, somebody having an epileptic seizure?"

"A what?"

"Like, somebody's in, like an airport, say, and all the sudden they just fall to the ground and start shaking. Like this."

She shakes her body around like she just stuck her finger in a light-bulb socket. I try not to laugh.

"Don't laugh. This is important. Okay, now. Do what I just did."

I hesitate.

"Member what I said. No naysaying."

"I feel stupid."

"Well, you're gonna feel real stupid by the side of the road, how's that?"

I do it real fast and keep doing it and don't stop till she's convinced, shaking my body this way and that, flopping round like a fish out of water.

"All right. All right, kid, I get the point. Now, what you're gonna do is, you're gonna look real sweet, act real nice and go into this little store. Alone. Now, while you're in front, I'm gonna be in the back, never mind why. Now, you have to do that, like shake like that and fall to the ground and keep shaking, for about two minutes. No more, no less. Got it? Count in your head if you have to."

I nod back, serious, not wanting to naysay my way out the car.

"Then, when two minutes are up, get off the floor, wipe yourself off like you're kinda still in a daze, smile sweet and say something like, 'Oh my goodness, what a scare, but I'm okay now, I'll be all right.' That kinda thing. And then you just put yourself together, walk right out, take a right and I'll be round the corner. Just get in real normal-like, and we'll drive off. Simple. Got it?"

"So, um, when're we gonna be doing this?"

"In about ten minutes."

"What?"

"What yourself. Is there a problem?"

"Um, just seems a little soon is all."

"Lookit, are you in or what?"

"Yeah, but . . . um, wull, where do you want me to do it?"

"Right in front of the counter. Just go up. Smile real sweet. Maybe ask for some bubble gum. And then, when he turns to get it, drop and shake. If you can drool from your mouth that'd be good, but I know it's hard to drool on command, maybe think of a lemon. Just remember, two minutes. Don't forget."

"Okay."

I'm starting to get nervous. If I blow it, she'll hate me, or worse, leave me behind. I bite my lip. The last thing I want is to get dumped by the side of the road.

"All right, so you got about five minutes to turn into little Miss Muffett. I got a comb and some barrettes back there somewhere, maybe in that yellow bag. So get to work."

I take out the yellow bag and start combing while I pick out two little pink barrettes with circus animals on top. Perfect. I put those in, pinch my cheeks till they're rosy, primp and preen some more. I'm starting to get terrified I won't live up. All my nervousness is turning into fussiness about my hair and my cheeks and my practice smile. My heart is pounding. Glenda just keeps smoking, cigarette after cigarette. She hunches into the steering wheel, bearing down into the road.

"You nervous, Glenda?"

She looks at me, in the mirror, caught.

"Hell no."

"Me neither."

"Course not."

But if you asked the air, it would tell you different. The back of the car swishes to a halt as we pull up onto the gravel next to a little yellow store with a wooden sign across the top saying, "Custer's Last Stand."

ELEVEN

I see myself in the store window as I walk across the gravel. You might as well put lipstick on a duck. Looks like I'm trying just a little too hard in my circus animal barrettes and Fruit Loop smile, just pink and goofy. You could dip me in plastic and sell me at the Toys-R-Us.

But I have a self-protection clause that says when I'm feeling down on my luck or sorry for myself or goofy or ugly or hopeless, I better just think about those bubble-bellied kids in Africa with nothing to eat but dirt for breakfast and flies buzzing around their faces, so used to it that they're just landing swat-free, cause what's the point in swatting, anyways, let alone living? If you start thinking about that, then you might as well be a superstar by comparison.

And now I remember to pretend that this is all just a movie and I am the number one star. There's nothing to be afraid of. It's not real. It's an act. It's a story. It's a dream of a life of some precocious teenage passion bomb, played by yours truly. Just watch how I giggle and wiggle and smile and nod.

The glass door crashes behind me and rattles me back to my next thought, which is, How the hell am I gonna pull this off? But I will not naysay myself into inaction. I will proceed as planned, by hook or by crook, more like crook, in my own private movie.

I clench my jaw and walk up to the counter, where an elbow-faced man of about one hundred and sixty years stands squinting at me. I flash my piggy smile and tilt my head like I'm an idiot.

"Hey there."

He smiles back. He is missing not one but two of his front teeth. There's a twinkle in his eye, though, like he's been standing there for fifty years without a customer, like he's used to being invisible and maybe doesn't exist at all.

"Do you have Hubba-Bubba?"

I hear myself talking like Minnie Mouse, like a cartoon version of myself. This is the way girls talk in movies, like they need help tying their shoelaces.

"Sure thing, pumpkin."

He winks and I turn my wince into a smile. I feel guilty. He seems like a nice man, pure kinda. Not like the sort of bad egg you want to pull a fast one on. I am starting to have second thoughts. The music to my movie is getting warbled and now the record is just about to scratch.

I steel myself. No naysaying. I can't hold out much longer so I make up my mind to just get it over with. I feel like rotten cotton candy.

"What flavor, Missy?"

"Watermelon," I say, too quick.

He fumbles around with his hands, using the counter for support, trying to rouse his ancient bones to turn and inspect the Hubba Bubba display. He looks like a man who's forgotten something. Puzzled. I wait for what seems like an eternity. With every millimeter he moves, my heart beats louder. By the time his back is to me it's not that hard to hit the deck and start shaking. I'm skittish on the inside so I just turn myself inside out and Bob's your uncle. My epileptic starring role comes perfectly natural. My heart feels like it's gonna pop right out of my chest smack-dab into the middle of the white tile floor.

The square tiles are cold under my back and I'm hitting them hard with my shoulder blades and elbows, getting carried away. I got to remember not to crack my own skull. You should see it, I am dedicated tooth and nail to this here show. I try to make spit come out the corner of my mouth. Think of a lemon. Think of a lemon, switching from a lemon to a sour-tart to a rhubarb pie and then back again. Finally my mouth starts to spill over with drool and I almost burst out giddy with my latest talent. This is really something. Boy, I am drooling now and I could not be more proud. I wish Glenda could see this. She'd be proud as punch. Tammy, too, she'd say, "Look at her go, I taught her everything she knows."

In the corner of my spastic eye, I see the old man waddling towards me, just as fast as a waddler can waddle. I see him in flashes through my strobe-light vision. He struggles down to his knees beside me, a Herculean effort, whispering something I can't understand. I see the fear in his eyes in bits and pieces. His shock is weird and contagious and makes my eyes pop open a second and then spaz around even more. He tries to grab me, but his toothpick arms are just too weak for a young epileptic like me. My cheeks and chin are covered in drool. I wiggle harder.

And then something strange happens. The whispering stops. The grabbing stops. The earth stops.

I sneak open my eyes to see what's the problem and nearly faint as I witness the last breath exhaled by this ancient creature, born before time and raised before television, as he covers his heart with his hand and keels over smack-bang on top of me.

TWELVE

Not exactly what I had in mind, kid."

She towers over me, staring at the picture I made for her. The old man slumps on top of me like a white rag doll.

"Get him off me." I grunt out, trying to lift off his flailing limbs but failing.

Glenda sighs and shoves him over, grabbing my hand and pulling me up towards the door.

"Nice work, kid. Now we're murderers."

"Is he dead?"

"I dunno. Fuck. This is not good."

She grabs me by the wrists and throws me out the door.

"Wull, maybe we better call someone or something . . ."

She's pulling me along the gravel, about as fast as heels can race-walk, dust flying up around our feet, like an angry steam engine churning. My arm feels like it's four feet in front of its socket and I look back to see if there happen to be any witnesses to our little travesty.

"Don't look back, kid. Just keep moving."

We turn the corner into the brush where the car's hidden between two side-by-side weeping willows, the rabbit waiting for us, impatient. Glenda hurls me into the back and jumps in the driver's seat. She fumbles around for the car keys, hands shaking, swearing little half words to herself, like she doesn't have time enough to finish them.

"We can't just leave him there." I say it.

"Oh yes we can."

"No we can't, Glenda."

"Amateur."

"Listen. Listen to me. You took money from that place, didn't you?"

"How'd you guess?"

"Wull, think about it. What looks weirder . . . two girls call an ambulance for some old guy who just dropped dead and oh they're so upset they called the cops right away, and then maybe two months later someone figures out some money happens to be missing . . . or . . . or . . . some old guy is dead behind the counter with no one in sight and there's some fucking money missing."

She stops fumbling.

I catch her eyes and say quiet, "Get it? It's better to just call the cops and play dumb."

She starts to work it over in her head. You might think this is me being good, but really this is me not wanting that old geezer knocking down the door to my peaceful slumbers trying to turn all my late-night dreaming into nightmares.

"You're right."

I breathe a sigh of relief. I do not want to take that old man with me to bed every night.

"You're right."

"Do you think he's dead?"

"I dunno. I dunno. Just shush. I gotta get organized here."

She hops out the car and hustles back into the store, searching behind the counter for the phone. I keep one step behind her, trying to pick up a few pointers. She finds the phone, stops herself, lets out a breath like she's communing with the gods and dials 911.

"Hello, hello . . . yes, um . . . we have an emergency here . . . we've got a, well, a dead or sick gentleman, here. I mean, he just sorta fell over mid-sentence down here at Custer's Last Stand . . . yep, down on Highway 92 . . . I swear to God you better hurry, maybe there's still hope. My name? My name is Cheryl. Cheryl Tarkington. Please do hurry. I just don't know what to do . . . I've got my daughter here and all, probably traumatized for life." She hangs up the phone and looks at me. "This better fucking work."

I look up at her, starting to question my decision. Maybe I'm wrong and am gonna spend the rest of my life in the slammer with girls named Lakeisha and Irma and Jean. I resign myself to live a life of study behind bars, like Malcolm X, emerging a prophet with the wisdom of my redemption.

Glenda clasps her hands. "Let's pray."

She and I stand side-by-side, heads down, and here's her prayer:

"Dear God, don't let that man die. Amen."

We wait a thousand years before two officers of the law come swaggering through the door, one white bread, one Mexican. The white bread one has hair the color of dishwater and blue eyes and a gait like he's about to fight off a bull. He looks Glenda over, up and down, and I can tell he likes what he sees. The Mexican cop stands by the front door, waiting for the ambulance, posing like there's a photographer in the bushes taking pictures for some hero calendar.

"Ma'am, you here when it happened?"

He's got a voice like a bass drum, like his throat got cut in two and now all that's coming out is pure man.

"Why, yes I was, and so was my daughter here, Isabel, and I am just so worried she'll be traumatized for life because of this, oh, you should have seen it, poor girl."

He looks down at me, some TV cop sent from Hollywood to play the role of gallant hunk.

"It's okay, darlin, these things happen, it's all part of the natural ebb and flow of life."

I nod, pretending to hide my lost innocence. Really I'm thinking he's damn good-looking for a cop. Glenda interrupts, laying on the honey.

"Are you sure you're old enough to be a cop? You look awful young to me."

He flushes a bit and takes off his hat, cowboy-style with a little police thrown in.

"I most assuredly am. And if I dare say, you don't look old enough to be her mother."

"Oh now." She fake-swats him and tilts her head to the side, blushing like a schoolgirl.

The Mexican cop gives a look over to his partner and turns back, shaking his head. I am taken aback at seeing Glenda in action. She's a pro, all right, and he is buying it wholesale. The ambulance pulls up to the front and a man and a woman come tumbling out, rushing to the old man, taking his pulse and stretching back his eyelids.

"Looks like there's life in him yet."

"No shit." White Bread scratches his head.

Glenda and I crane in, looking for some hope, any hope, that'll slow our too-quick drop to hell. Please God, don't kill him. Not on our watch. Please, not today.

They start buzzing around him, flashing a light in his eyes, taking his pulse. Boy oh boy, he sure knows how to be old, this one. It's like you could snap him in two just by looking at him. Right now they're trying to blow life into him but he sure is taking his time.

White Bread doesn't care, though, his eyes stay glued on Glenda and she keeps batting hers back at him. You'd think they were at the homecoming bonfire instead of standing in front of the counter with a half-dead old gummer square on the tiles between.

The ambulance paragons lift the man onto the gurney, shaking their heads and conferring.

"Looks like you best be headed straight to Campbell ER," the Mexican cop chimes in, not sounding Mexican at all.

"That's your best bet. Best ER in the state," he adds, matter-of-fact.

But White Bread ain't listening. He's just leaning into Glenda, eyes swirling. He turns his back to the Mexican cop and whispers in, "Hey, listen, you got a phone number or something? Maybe I could call you and we could go have a drink somewhere, when I'm off duty, just talk."

"Just talk, eh?"

Glenda gives him a sideways smile and you can feel his temperature rise inside his body.

The ambulance doors slam and the Mexican cop waves back, giving them a thumbs-up sign, TV-ready. They drive off into the distance, siren singing them off into greener pastures. The Mexican cop turns to his partner, looking none too pleased.

"Well, Mike, we better shut this place down and get a move on. Your *wife* might be mighty angry with you if you're late for dinner two nights in a row."

White Bread looks down at the floor, sure annoyed, but keeping his cool. Glenda picks all this up, mulls it around and runs with it.

"Your *wife?* Well, maybe I won't be giving you my number after all, you naughty boy, leading me on like that."

She gives White Bread a little pout. He gives his partner a look like he's gonna take him straight out back and kick his ass right there in the brambles. Then he turns back to Glenda, giving a little shrug.

"Well, ma'am, maybe next lifetime."

Glenda smiles back, coy and twinkling. "Maybe so."

She grabs my hand and marches out the door. Before we round the bend she looks back and blows a kiss, can you believe it, blows a kiss, and sways her way back into the car.

I climb into the back seat, behind the bunny rabbit. Glenda shuts the door gently, picks up the keys, starts the car and drives off real slow and smooth, like some shark swimming casual away from its kill. Two miles down the blacktop she looks straight ahead and decides to speak.

"I'd say that went well."

THIRTEEN

Somewhere between Oshkosh and Lisco the old man starts knocking. I try not to let him in, but his skinny little fingers keep wrapping themselves round the door. Glenda seems to be coming down from her drugstore triumph. Something in her starts sinking fast and her knuckles stay white on the wheel. I wonder if he's knocking on her door, too.

"Glenda, do you think that—"

"No talking till we get to Wyoming."

She shoots me a look like she means it and catches the doubt written all over my forehead in little lines. She softens up a bit and pats the front of my seat.

"You did good, kid. All except the stroke part."

"Do you think he's gonna make it?"

"Sure he is."

"I mean, it wasn't my fault. He just had like a temporary stroke or something and went into a coma and he'll be fine in an hour maybe, right, don't you think—"

"Look, there's no use dwelling on it. Okay? He'll be fine. Just fine."

Silence.

"You heard the man. Campbell's got the best ER in the state. Hell, I even heard of Campbell. It's a famous establishment. Very famous."

Yup. He's been knocking on her door, too.

"But, what about—"

"Drop it."

"I mean, what if—"

"I said drop it."

I get the picture and slump down into my seat.

"Look, make me a cigarette, kid, and quit dwelling"

She nods towards the row of cigarettes on the dash. I lean up and reach across the seat. I pick one out, light it and slip it between her fingers. She nods her acceptance, takes it and keeps looking forward, furrowing her brow, somewhere between determination and fear.

I fumble with the radio.

"No music."

She checks the rearview and checks again, her hands glued to the wheel. Her dread is starting to seep over into the back seat. I look back at the blacktop. The sun is starting to go down and the sky is turning orange behind us, as if we set that world on fire and can barely make it down the road before getting burned ourselves. We drive through the stillness like there's a spell cast on everything except us, some frozen thing, waiting and watching from the fields. I stare silent into the turning light, trying to slam the door on that old man's fingers, creeping up, slamming and creeping up again.

I don't feel struck or sad or sinful. I just feel numb, thinking about that purple rag-doll stare above me, crushing my shoulder blades down into the cold tile floor. It doesn't seem real. It seems like some made-up schoolyard fantasy you'd try to dazzle your friends with before the bell. But when I look at Glenda's knuckles clenching the steering wheel, I know it's real. I know it's real and I know I can't go back. And if that old man don't make it, well, there's a piece of me that'll be left in that little store, too. There'll be this piece of me that no matter what I do, even if I return, even if I inspect every inch of every corner of that tile floor on my hands and knees for days, I will never, ever, get back.

I stare out the window as the stars come on one by one. I can't sleep. I beg Glenda to play music but she won't budge. She is hunched over the steering wheel like a vulture, peering into the big black night.

"What about if—"

"Okay, look, kid, I'm gonna let you in on a little secret and listen up cause this one'll get you through. You listening?"

"Yeah."

"Good. Okay, there's a trick you can do, okay? There's a trick you do when you start doing what you're doing now, which is dwelling. You're dwelling. You're stuck. Feel it? You're stuck. You're playing that same song over and over again about how he's gonna die and why me why me and you've got that song playing on repeat, am I right or am I right?"

"Yeah."

"Okay, now, I want you to put a quarter in the jukebox and change the record. Got it? You just change that record you got playing to a new song, okay? Find a different song. Something bright. Make it a good one and play that. Just change the record."

She looks my way and I try to pretend to get it. I try to, but honest, I ain't sure.

"That's lesson three."

"Can we turn on the radio?"

"Once we get to Wyoming."

Great.

It is the answer to everything. Can we play music? Once we get to Wyoming. Can we count our money? Once we get to Wyoming. Can I talk yet? Once we get to Wyoming.

It is our salvation, the light at the end of the tunnel, the pot of gold at the end of the rainbow. Wyoming.

Once we get to Wyoming, then we'll be happy.

FOURTEEN

Somewhere in the middle of the dark night and dreaming, Glenda lets out a squeal of delight and I am awakened from my crumpled daze.

"Seven lonely days makes one lonely week . . ."

She is singing at the top of her lungs, speeding along, smiling like she just won the Pillsbury Bake-Off.

"Seven lonely days makes one lonely—"

"Ha ha! Hey kid, we made it. We made it! C'mere, kid. I wanna give you a kiss."

I lean forward and she grabs me by the arm and kisses my hand, clumsy.

"Nice work, kid. You deserve an Academy Award from all those jack-offs in Hollywood. Now, I know it's not much, not an Oscar, mind you, but here's your cut. One thousand smackers. Don't spend it all in one place."

She winks and I look up at her, rumpled and speechless.

"That's right kid, for only $9.95 you, too, can flop all over the ground, have an ol geezer go black on top of you and still make out like a bandit! For not one, not two, but one thousand smackers you, too, can be the pride of your hometown and flip the Joneses the bird."

She's floating above me now, cackling, smiling, singing, smoking. She starts rubbing off on me, too. She was right. We're safe now.

We're in Wyoming.

"There you go, kid." She hands me a wad of cash in a rubber band.

I look down at my cut like someone just dropped a cockroach in the middle of my palm. This is not what I was expecting. I thought I was just the bait. Not the sidekick.

"One thousand even. Count it. Exactly half. Down the line. You and me. Half and half. The actress and the thief. That sounds like the name of a movie. The actress and the thief. One of us would have to be a boy, though. So we could make out. Nobody wants to see a movie where people don't make out. Anyway, you did good, kid. I'm proud of you. Next stop, we'll get something to eat. Maybe drink, too. I could use a drink. Shit. You like whiskey?"

"No."

"Holy shit! How old are you?"

"Thirteen."

"Thirteen!"

"Yup."

"Don't like whiskey?"

"Nope."

"What are you, some kinda communist?"

"Nope."

"This country's going to hell in a handbasket."

"Sorry."

"I mean, that's downright un-American."

I nod my agreement and stash the wad of cash in my fancy stole bag.

"Tell you what, first things first. We'll stop. We'll have one drink and then we'll go get something to eat. I think it's appropriate that we celebrate first, don't you? I mean, we can't have you pulling heists without a whiskey and Coke toast."

"Whiskey and Coke?" Great. I get to be a drunk now, too.

"Oh, by the way, you've got money now. So you're gonna have people on your ass, hounding you, trying to get it outta you. A fool and his money are easy to part. So you gotta learn. You gotta learn how to read people. You gotta figure out their angle. Cause everybody's got an angle. Everybody. So from now on I don't wanna see anymore bending and shuffling and hemming and hawing. Unless it's an act. Then that's okay. But otherwise, you gotta stand up straight and look people in the eye. You gotta see what they're hiding. Lesson four."

I nod back at her, taking it in, imagining myself outwitting grifters.

"You scared?"

"Nope."

"You wanna go back?"

"Nope."

"Good. Who knows? You may be some kinda disguised blessing."

We pull into a truck stop that's got a bowling alley shooting out the back, attached to a bar. It's got white chip paint with a red stripe going horizontal, all the way around. There's a neon sign above flashing, "Blane's Lanes," with the B flickering on and off from "Blane's Lanes" to "lane's Lanes" and then back again.

I take the circus animal barrettes out of my hair and try to look sophisticated. I am no sucker. Not anymore. I'm a sidekick. You can't fool me no more. Glenda hands me her lipstick, ruby red. I put it on, smack my lips and tossle up my hair, like that girl on Remington Steele.

Glenda powders her nose, lights a cigarette and looks my way.

"Welcome to Lusk, kid."

FIFTEEN

We walk in and they look at us like we've got rabies. It looks like the Fifties in here, orange and white with gold sprucing up the place for good measure. The bartender looks up, sees Glenda and starts shaking his head, playful. There are two fat guys sitting side by side at the bar, both in flannels with red noses like they've been drinking since breakfast. At the end of the bar, a skinny Mexican boy with big brown eyes sits drinking a Shasta. He peers at us over the counter, his chin resting on the bar, tilted to one side, quizzical.

"You better fix your B before someone starts calling you Lane." Glenda says it.

"They already do."

The bartender looks me up and down. He has salt-and-pepper hair and piercing green eyes. I can't bring myself to look at him. He looks like the kind of guy who could break up a fight, change a tire and spoon-feed his dying mother, all at once. He moves slow and doesn't bend over himself or hunker down.

Glenda gives him a side smile and makes a point of perusing the abandoned lanes. There's a silence between these two. Like no one wants to show his hand.

"Tell him your name, kid."

I try to look up at him but end up looking at the bar.

"Luli."

"What's that again?"

"My name's Luli."

"Hmmph. That's a new one. Well, my name's Blane. Pleased to meet ya."

Glenda's watching me now, taking notes. Later she'll tell me what I did wrong, where I blew it and not to tell my name to the barstool.

"Well, Blane, you gonna stand there gawking or you gonna pour us a drink? Me and the kid, here, got some celebrating to do."

Blane looks at the little Mexican boy and makes a sign with his hand. The boy laughs. Blane nods and looks back at me. The boy grins and I look away.

"Cat got your tongue?" I say, real smart.

"He's mute, Luli."

For the first time, I see something new in Glenda, something like quietness and resignation and wanting to fix the world but feeling helpless.

"Got a present for ya, kid." Glenda hands the keys to me. "Go get the you-know-what outta the car, Luli."

"The what?"

"You know." She leans in and whispers, "The bunny."

"Oh! Oh, yeah, okay, gotcha."

I go out to the car, open the door and start wrestling with the bunny in the dark. His ear gets trapped in the seatbelt, and I'm feeling pretty stupid playing outsmart with a stuffed rabbit in the middle of the parking lot. Finally I get my grip and start lugging the bunny across the dirt. It's cumbersome and unwieldy and everything else you don't want to do after a long day of faking epileptic fits and old men keeling over. His bunny feet are dragging on the ground, getting dusty, and I'll probably be getting bitched at for that, too.

I push the door open with my back and hoist the bunny over beside the Mexican boy. Glenda looks on with pride as I prop the thing up next to him, facing him in some button-eyed greeting. Blane starts to chuckle. He and Glenda seem to have some private moment of unspoken meaning that goes back to before I was born.

I look at the mute Mexican boy. He inspects the bunny, smiles. Then he points to himself, crosses his chest and points back at me. Then he does it again. And again. I pretend not to notice. I pretend to fix my shirt. I pretend not to get it. Glenda looks at my made-up shirt-fixing and then back at the boy.

"Well, well. Looks like you got yourself an admirer here, Luli."

I pretend to inspect the tile floor.

Blane pours two whiskey Cokes, watches the boy and looks back at me.

"I believe he's trying to say he loves you."

The two fat flannels take notice and start laughing. One of them sputters out, "Looks like that bunny rabbit sure did the trick. Ha ha ha."

The other one slaps him on the back, laughing hard and mean.

The Mexican boy keeps signing away, harder this time. Point. Cross. Point. Stop. Point. Cross. Point. And then again. Glenda starts chuckling along with the two flannels. Blane grins, joining in. They laugh and look over to me for an answer, expectant.

I hesitate, mortified. If you could see my cheeks they'd be lobster-colored. I try to think of something clever, something to get the staring off me, something to separate me from the Mexican boy, to keep him and his affliction at bay. I have to swat him away before I catch whatever it is he caught that makes you have to talk with your hands.

"You know, it's funny." I say, starting up. "You may not believe it, but I picked up some sign language myself, here and there, along the way."

And here I start my barrage of international hand signals for "Fuck you." I start with the simple finger, then the flick off the chin, then the thumb to the nose with wavy fingers, then the arm-cross and then back to the finger. I repeat these gestures, going faster each time. I start directing them around the room, sporadic, at Blane, Glenda and the two flannels. Blane starts to laugh and the rest follow suit. I'm in. I've won them over. I've put myself far, far away from any malady I can catch from that mute.

But the Mexican boy ain't laughing. He looks red-eyed and stung. Luckless. He turns away and then bolts out the back.

There's a silence now. The flannels shrug, going back to their beer. Glenda lights a cigarette. Blane turns towards me.

"Go apologize."

I look to Glenda for credit. She stares into her whiskey, jingling the ice around like she's waiting for a train. One of the flannels chuckles silently into his beer.

"Go apologize."

Glenda raises an eyebrow, swivels her seat towards me and says, "It's your call, kid."

"Goddamnit, Glenda!" Blane slams his glass down onto the bar hard and stares at her, looking straight through to the back of her head.

"That little boy's got a name. You didn't even tell her his name. He's got a name, you know." He turns to me and says real clear, "His name's Angel. He's not deaf. He's not dumb. He can think like you or me. He has feelings like you or me. He just can't talk is all. So don't treat him like a fucking retard."

He starts to calm down a little, wiping the sweat off his brow. He turns back to Glenda. "Now I don't know who your little playmate is, here, but she made quite an impression. And I want you to tell her to go apologize."

"Look, Blane, I brought him that fucking bunny all the way from Memphis, now just cool your jets about it—"

"Tell her."

Glenda doesn't look at me. She stares back through him, blowing smoke in his face, keeping cold.

"Luli, go apologize."

Whatever this spider web is I've walked into, it has nothing to do with me. These looks, this staring, goes back. This is part of some unspoken rambling going back to before time. Just another fight and looky-me, thrown in the center. I feel right at home.

I grab the bunny rabbit round the waist and drag it across the floor and out the back. I can hear the flannels snickering as the screen door slams behind me. Outside, the air smells sweet and the grasshoppers hum so loud it's like they're gonna take over.

They buzz and buzz like they're some unseen electric army chuffing themselves up for war.

There's a run-down, gray-white, one-room house sitting off to the side of the dirt patch behind the alley. Angel sits on the front porch, leaning sideways on the rail, his body bent into a lower-case r. He sees me come out but doesn't bother to turn his neck. He looks at the moon glowing orange, low in the sky. Harvest moon. Indian summer. The leaves outside fixing to turn red, orange, yellow and then throw themselves off the trees. They got about a month to meet their maker.

Here's the thing I didn't notice before. He's tall, more intimidating than I'd clocked inside. He dwarfs me, which ain't hard to do. But I thought he was younger or smaller or less to contend with.

I set the rabbit up against the steps and start kicking the gravel around at my feet, playing playful. He doesn't bite. I lean against the other railing, both of us facing out to the moon. The grass-hoppers hum through the silence, plotting their attack while we sit weak.

"That's a harvest moon."

He doesn't say nothing. The grasshoppers buzz and buzz again. He starts dragging his shoes through the gravel, a little at a time and then more, in a pattern. I look down and suss out he's writing some such. He finishes and it says, spelled out in gravel, "I'm mute. Not dumb."

I laugh. He smiles a little bit, not wanting to give in too easy.

"You know, Angel's a good name for you. You kinda look like an angel, like a Mexican angel."

I don't have to lie or coddle or butter it up. It's true. He's big-eyed and dark, stick skinny, like he's been working dawn to dusk since you could get work out of him. He's got muscles but they're tucked away, twined beneath and around the bone.

"Look. I'm sorry if I made you mad. I didn't mean to. I was just trying to make an impression or something back there. I dunno. I mean, I never met anyone who couldn't talk before and I guess I got a little spooked."

He writes again in the dirt, finishes and looks up. It says, "BOO."

"Ha ha. Very funny."

We both sit there, leaning on our respective railings, looking out into the grasshopper hum and the night air, hay sweet, the moon so close, like you could reach out and freeze your fingers.

I want to apologize to him for his made-silent life. I want to ask him why. I wonder why some people get to have the world on a string and others come up with a shit sandwich and dirt for dessert. I want to make it better. There's something about him that reminds me of my dad, helpless and still, like the air around him has to be gentle or he just might break.

"Luli!"

Glenda interrupts, swaggering out the back, framing herself mid-circle inside the moon.

"Hope you don't mind sleeping on the couch cause we ain't leaving."

She throws my bag at my feet and points inside. She turns to Angel.

"Blane said for you to make up a bed on the couch. You can sleep on the floor or make Luli sleep on the floor, either way."

She struts around, heads back, sensing my hesitation.

"Well. Git. Git going."

"You sure, Glenda? Cause maybe we could—"

"Is there a problem?"

"No, it's just—"

"Well, good, cause you know I don't like naysayers."

"Yeah, um, me neither."

"That's what I thought."

Angel heads inside the gray shack. Glenda strides back into the bowling alley. She starts laughing hard, cracking a joke. I sit there a moment, trying to get a fix on this new situation, Glenda's bag of tricks thrown at me on the fly. I check my money in my fancy bag. Still there. I decide to trust in Glenda and the end of the day and Indian summer, most of all, and make my way over the rickety porch inside.

I saunter into what looks like the living room and find it immaculate clean. Everything inside looks like it's been waiting here since the Forties, placed pristine and never moved. There's white lace doilies on the tables and Old West kerosene lamps. From the middle of the wall a cattle skull stares down in the moonlight. The wooden floor is covered with an old-style rug, trodden and ancient, burgundy battered into gray. That skull looks like it's just waiting for you to ask for directions.

Angel is putting the finishing touches on my makeshift bed, preening a bit, making it extra-special. I watch him start to make up his own bed on the floor, far less careful. I guess I get the good quilt.

"You don't have to sleep on the floor. I'll take the floor. I don't mind."

He doesn't respond and, instead, lays purposeful down on the floor, tucking himself snug under the quilt. He turns away from me, closing his eyes.

It seems early to go to bed, but I guess when in Rome do whatever. I lay down in my good quilt bed and stare at the ceiling. Glenda's bar laugh drifts through the wood-panel walls. The crickets keep planning their attack, softer now, getting sneaky. There's a little breeze, crisp, like fall's sending its regards from the sidewalk before stepping across the threshold. I close my eyes and try to bury the day.

I get woke by a weird stillness. There's a quiet now, a pitch black hovering. Then I realize that Angel has crept up next to me, kneeling beside me on the floor. I pretend not to see him. I make believe I'm still asleep, curious.

He sits over me, staring underneath the blanket. He's looking at me like I'm made of crystal, a new invention.

I half-hearted toss and turn, throwing the quilt over my eyes so I can peek through the yarn without him knowing. His eyes swirl in the moonlight. We stay this way for a long time.

Finally, just as I'm about to sleep or move or speak, he reaches his hand out and touches my bare skin. I stay still. He looks at me, tentative, wondering if I'll wake. My stillness is near impossible to maintain. I try not to move a muscle.

I want to see what comes next.

He moves his hand down my arm and onto my thigh. Then he stops and looks at me, checking. So far, so good. He traces my leg down towards my ankles. Again, he looks at me. Again, I play dead.

And I don't know why I let him, but I do. Maybe I just like watching myself, strange and quiet and real. There's a suspense to it, like the music just got spooky. Even the crickets outside are hushed up and waiting.

He moves his hand up the inside of my leg. He stops and looks, making sure. I hold my breath. He moves his hand up over my hipbones and over my chest. His fingers are shaking. His movement is awkward, boy-like, fragile.

He stops, staring at me. He runs his fingers over the pink part, making an outline, tracing. I hold my breath.

The bar door slams, outside, breaking the moment in two. Then a fall. Then a cackle. Glenda reels in Blane's arms, the gravel crunching beneath their feet.

Angel recoils to his position on the floor, guilty.

The front door slams shut behind Glenda, tipsy. Blane leads her to his room, quiet, slow, concerned. He closes the door gently behind.

Angel stares up at the ceiling, bothered.

I turn away now. Tired. Wondering. Exhausted by my thoughts and the endlessness of the day. The crickets turn back on, lulling me to sleep.

In the morning, we leave. Just like that. We leave without saying good-bye or coffee cups or anything. Glenda just wakes me up and we're out in five minutes. And this is what I like about Glenda. This is what makes me want to stand next to her and jump inside her. She always knows when to leave and how. She knows how to read the silence and the pause between words. She knows what happens on the other side of walls and under good quilts in the dark.

And I know, somehow, she knew. Like clockwork.

She knew.

SIXTEEN

So, tell the truth, kid, and be honest. How'd ya leave it? Am I gonna see you on the back of one of them milk cartons? Cause I wanna be prepared."

The Wyoming sky is flying past us, Indian summer setting fire to the sky. Up ahead phantom squiggles billow up in waves off the pavement. I'm tired of driving, tired of moving. I'm still back in that shack with Angel touching me in the quiet, thinking about hands in the dark and pink parts and eyes swirling.

I want to stop. I want to get a hold of the world and stop it turning. I want to walk into a bar and see my dad. I want him to pull up a chair next to me and tell a dumb joke. I want him to scruff up my hair and make pretend he just pulled off my nose. I want him to look at Glenda, fall for her, forget about Tammy giggling late night behind the bar. I want him to be young again. Happy.

The truth is, maybe someday I will run into him and maybe he'll even recognize me, all grown up. Maybe he'll see me at the end of the bar and remember that long lost girl he ran off from for a little while and then a little longer and then for good.

But I know he's drowning. He's out there somewhere, maybe even not that far away, maybe in the next town, maybe in that honky-tonk two towns back. Staring into his ice clinking. Silent. Brooding. Plotting his revenge, half-hearted. Stumbling out the bar, dazed. And maybe even some lady, some aging beauty queen, will take pity on him. He'll sleep in her bed and she'll try to solve the mystery of his silence. She'll wait, patient, contemplating his stone-faced nature, trying to unlock the key, hoping someday this quiet will, miraculous, transform itself into love, hoping someday he'll look at her and draw his hand up her dress, pushing her against the kitchen wall. Falling.

Something in him is letting go, giving up, surrendering.

I can feel it.

He won't go back. I know it. Why would he? She doesn't want him around anymore. She'd rather push him off a cliff than have him gaze up at her smitten. She doesn't want to look at him and be reminded that she can't love him back. She doesn't want to look at him and think about how she could have done better. She doesn't want to look at him and think about that baby boy she once had, almost had, born blue.

I have a secret daydream that I see my dad. I play it over and over and over again. Do you know how long it lasts? How long does love last? How can it be that she gets to go on snickering, chortling through her days and nights, while he sits, sinking slow down into the rocks, seeing the world like looking up from the bottom of a fishbowl. Looking up through the water, the light refracting, unfocused, from somewhere above, a blur of something that used to be.

I know he'll never get up.

"Luli?"

"Huh?"

"Do you think your mom's gonna be looking for you?"

That's a new thought. I never looked at it like that. I never imagined Tammy would miss me. I know how she sees me. I make her feel guilty. I remind her that she's supposed to be in love with my dad. I remind her that she got old. I remind her that I'm the one left. I'm the one that made it.

"No."

"You sure?"

"Yup."

"Cause I don't want any trouble, not that kind, not like I kidnapped you or something or made you do something against your will . . ."

The road tumbles by beneath us.

"Do you have any more of that stuff in that vial or whatever?"

Glenda looks at me, wary.

"Sure, kid, have at it."

I keep staring at the road, not sure what to make of my new dark mood. Maybe I could just let it pass or pretend it's not there or sweep it under the rug like my expert mama. Maybe I could just open this door and tumble out underneath the wheels and that would be that, finally, for good.

It's not just that he's stuck somewhere, my dad, or dead in a ditch, covered in dirt, with a sad song playing in the background.

It's not even that I'll never see him again. It's that even if I did see him, even if my best dream came true and I walked into some red shoebox bar with Elvis crooning behind and there he was, clinking his 7 & 7, even if he looked up at me, remembered me and even smiled, even if all that happened . . . it would still mean more to me, a thousand times more, than it ever would to him.

I'm that kid he had, accidental and unimportant, like dropping your keys on the way out the door. I'm something that happened that doesn't really matter much now, some dwarf version of the woman he loves who can't love him back. And when he looks at me, he thinks of her, all moonlight and memory. He thinks of the first time she saw him, the first time she looked back at him and from somewhere, the corner of her eye or the middle of her mouth, let him see her sparkle. She knows how to make herself sparkle.

And he'll think about how in that moment, behind the bar, two blocks over, the train went running over the tracks, hustling to get to the next hick town, and how he felt like the tracks were inside him, running through him, as his heart raced and she tossed her hair and looked over her shoulder and sparkled bright. She liked to let him look at her like that. She liked to twinkle her eyes and watch him swoon.

But if I did that, if I tried to put a twinkle in my eye and giggle and sprinkle sparkle dust, it would be like yelling in a forest, lost and who cares anyways.

That's the difference.

So it's not that he's dead and dramatic and weighty and meaningful. It's not that. It's that he doesn't care, pure and simple. It's that he made me and watched me grow and taught me how to talk and what to say and don't say too much, that he did all that, but that to him it was like having a pet, some fuzzy broken thing you found whining through the window in winter and decided to take under your wing.

Except now that she's gone, now that that house and that memory and that time and that window, now that all these things are crumpled up like an old newspaper, who cares about some fuzzy broken thing you took a shine to in sparklier days? Back then you would've saved a dying rat if it cried pathetic enough, looking up at you with those beady little eyes.

That's the difference.

To me it's all longing and wishing and knowing in my heart that my impossible dream will never become a reality. To him it's like picking a piece of lint off your shirt sleeve, something you might look at for a second but then never think twice about.

"Grab my purse, if you wanna, in the back." Glenda crashes my personal dirge.

She reaches into the backseat behind and tosses her purse on my lap, keeping eyes on the road. Now that the bunny's gone, I'm promoted to front seat. I look at her concentrating on the road, from my newfound shotgun, and wonder if there's someone she thinks about like this, someone quiet and massive who can change her day if she lets herself think too much.

Does she have it, too, some lonely, empty space that sits in the hollow of her chest, changing with the weather like some kind of never-say-so condition? And if she had it, if she had that permanent condition of the heart, what would she do with it? Where would she put it? I want to know. I want to know because I want to put it there, too.

I reach down and start sorting through her purse, bit by bit. I find the white powder vial, untwist the top and lift it up to my nose, breathing in. It burns like metal and creeps down the back of my throat. I shake my head and stare into the visor mirror, feeling better, hoping that the feeling lasts, watching the sun raise itself to the top of the sky.

I am made of steel now. Metallic. Numb.

Maybe this is the place you put it.

SEVENTEEN

Glenda doesn't know I have a .45.

And I'm not gonna tell her. How can I when so much has gone on with me keeping it secret? If I confess now, she'll wonder why I kept it from her so long and what I'm up to anyways. She'll think I'm hiding something else.

No, it's best not to tell her. It'll just make her wonder if she should have picked me up in the first place.

It'll just be my little secret.

EIGHTEEN

By the time we pull into Jackson, I feel a hundred years older and fifty pounds too heavy, like I have rocks in my shoulders. Glenda pulls up to a ranch-style house with a slate-stone sidewalk winding up. You have to walk through an oriental-looking garden, complete with miniature waterfalls spilling out over into little lily-padded fish ponds. It's real neat and tidy, like they hire a maid each Tuesday to dust off the leaves and polish the ceramic frogs.

A lumbering ox of a man comes out the front door like he's walking onstage on one of those late-night shows, expectant and smiley, waiting to bask in thunderous applause. Sensing no takers, he hulks towards us with big outstretched arms. I stop and pretend to look at the shiny green frogs, newly dusted, staring up, while I wait for Glenda to catch up and interact with Mr. Rogers over there. I take note that some of the fish in the little ponds are gold, some are white and gold and some are just see-through sickly white like they're radioactive and are just about two inbred laps from swimming to that great end-of-the-line fish tank.

Glenda grabs me by the back of the neck and turns me towards Mr. Friendly, who's well over six feet and two feet wide. He picks me up before I can get out of it and gives me a big bear hug like he's gonna crack my ribs with kindness. I turn my cringe into a squiggly-mouth smile till he relents, finally, putting me down.

"This here's Lloyd, Luli," Glenda chimes out round the cigarette she's squinting into, trying to light up in the afternoon breeze.

"Luli! We-hell, that sure is a funny name for a little filly."

I stare at his feet, which happen to be wrapped up in beige snakeskin cowboy boots. He's got on brown pants, a brown cowboy shirt and a tan Stetson hat. He takes up the whole top step.

Glenda nudges me.

"Um, wull, my name was supposed to be Lucy, but I couldn't say it, I just kept saying Luli, so they just gave up tryin."

"That so? Well, good thing your name wasn't Elizabeth."

He says this like it's the punch line and neither Glenda or I know quite what to make of it. We stand there, watching him, trying to figure it out. He keeps on smiling, big and stupid.

I try to compensate.

"I like your fishes, Mister."

"Mister! Look, just call me Lloyd, that's my name."

All this affection is making me nervous. In my house we didn't even hug each other on Christmas, let alone be nice to each other, and we certainly didn't hug complete strangers fresh off the street. I figure he's up to something. Either that or he just doesn't know me well enough to figure out that I'm not worth the trouble.

He invites us in and grabs Glenda by the hand, tugging her towards him. Just as we're about to reach the threshold, Glenda turns to me and whispers, real serious and mean, "Don't fuck this up."

Then she smiles and glides through the door with the greatest of ease.

NINETEEN

We walk in and the first person I see is Eddie Kreezer. He meets my surprise with a surly nod, as if he's seen it all before. I am waiting for Glenda to hit the deck but she doesn't even give him a second glance. She's acting like she knew he'd be there all along, or if she didn't, she's not about to let on that it bothers her. Lloyd points the bar out to me like a proud parent.

"You see that, Luli? I made it myself. Picked out the wood. Put in the mirrors. Hell, I musta went to every garage sale in Wyoming just to get those signs. Authentic."

The bar is filled with flashing beer signs, some ancient, some shiny. There's a blue-and-silver ball hanging from the ceiling with some horses lined up in a circle around the outside. When the ball spins the horses jump up and down. Lloyd sees me looking at it and flips a switch. The ball lights up, revealing its secret: Pabst Blue Ribbon. Behind the ball is the mirrored back wall, with swirls running through the mirror tiles to make it look like marble. The bar and the stools look like padded leather, but when I sit down they feel more like plastic.

Glenda and Eddie are staring at each other like they're connected by an invisible string and, if either of them moves, the house is gonna explode. Lloyd winks at me as he mixes the drinks.

"So, Luli, you like whiskey?"

I look at Glenda for a hint. She ignores me. She's looking through Eddie like he's made of glass and he's looking right back. I wonder how long this little staring contest is gonna last.

"No sir, I'm a little too young for that, I guess."

"You guess?"

"Yes sir."

Lloyd bursts out laughing and hands me a drink.

"Liar. I was drinking whiskey when I was ten. Drink up. That's a 7 & 7. You know what that is? 7-Up and Seagram's 7. That's why they call it 7 & 7, see. Perfect for starting up. I think I'll have one myself." He smiles real big and raises his glass. "Bottoms up."

He throws his drink back and slams it on the table, fixing to refill. I just sit there, sipping and looking over my glass at the weirdo dynamic on the other side of the room.

Lloyd raises his glass again, topped off, and says, "Skull." He drinks up and whispers to me, "That's what they say in Norway."

I nod, trying to care.

Lloyd motions towards Eddie with his glass. "See there, that's my son." He pauses for effect. "Well, not really my son, but like my son. Right, Eddie?"

Eddie stays looking at Glenda, frozen and electric.

"Right." The corners of his mouth creep into a tight smile. "Dad."

Glenda storms into the other room like that was a direct insult. Eddie starts laughing.

"Boy, what's gotten into her?" He gets up and stands next to me at the bar, facing Lloyd. "Bartender, give me a shot of tequila. On second thought, just give me the whole bottle."

He grabs the bottle off the bar, unscrews the top and tilts it back. He gulps down and looks at me, over his shoulder, acknowledging me for the first time.

"Sorry I pushed you outta my truck, kid." He takes another swig. "It's just . . . you make me nervous."

Then he heads out the front, bottle in hand.

Lloyd and I stare at the front door, wide open. Outside the sky is bright blue like a postcard for Wyoming. Wish you were here.

But right now I wish I wasn't here, what with the staring and the midday boozing and the smiling and the too-quick hugging.

Lloyd puts his arm around me, firm. He acts the way the good ol dads act on TV, warm and protective. He leads me through the sliding glass door and into the back. There's a pool set in concrete, with two lawn chairs and a table off to the side. Other than that, there's mostly just a couple of weeds and no real boundary between the backyard perimeter and the rest of the world. It just drops off from the pool and concrete into wilderness, which in this case is a burnt grassy plain scooping up into a hill.

"You like swimming, Luli?"

"Yes sir. Yes I do."

I am just itching to get into that blue sunshine water and wash the day off in one blue splash.

"Well, get in."

He grabs my drink and pushes me into the pool, clothes and everything. I don't know whether I'm supposed to laugh or take offense. I come up from the water and turn back to him.

"Thanks, Mister."

"Oh, now, c'mon. Just playin a little. Look, swim all you want, make yourself at home. I'll be inside with my sweet honey-bride. Hah, poet and didn't even know it."

Boy, he sure knows how to be a jackass.

He turns and walks inside, leaving me to wonder if by bride he meant Glenda and, if so, why she has so plainly neglected to mention the fact that she's married. And, especially, to this guy.

He looks back, calling out from the sliding door, "Oh, and Luli, there ain't a soul around here for miles."

He winks and slides the door closed, waving from inside the glass.

Weirdo.

I stay there, treading water, wondering what the hell Glenda has got me into here. I duck my head underwater and swim to the deep end. When I come up for air, Eddie appears from God knows where. He looks down at me, snide, hovering above. The sun shines bright behind, turning him black.

"Well, you heard what the man said. 'Nobody for miles.'"

He chuckles to himself, knocking back the tequila, pretending it's all a big funny joke. I stay there, frozen, squinting up at the sun like some kind of teenage tadpole.

"Not a soul, kid. I guess you could count me, but I think it might be debatable whether or not I count as a soul." He takes another swig. "You know what? I think you like me."

Oh Lord, here goes.

"Yeah, right." I laugh it off.

"I think you find me . . . worthy of note."

"Worthy of note?"

"You know . . . exciting."

He smiles, skinny, burning a hole in my eyes.

TWENTY

I swim to the shallow end and get out, trying to act casual. But I'm stumbling over my feet now, tripping my way over towards the house. Behind me Eddie's staring straight through me to somewhere beneath my skin. Something like shame is rustling up inside me, blushing and quivering, shaking me into feeling guilt for God knows what. I grab the screen door and try to slide it open. It's locked.

I turn around, expecting to see Eddie there, caught up and clawing. But instead of fangs and a full moon with lightning, he's just sitting there on the other side of the pool, Indian-style, not even looking my way. I try the door again, no luck, and make my way over the crabgrass to the front. Halfway there, I hear noises from inside the house, strange and stilted, like someone's trying to move a dresser. I peek in one of the windows, hiding in the curtain shade.

It's dark inside and I can barely see her. It's that late-afternoon light creeping into night, where the outside's yellow bright but the inside's getting ready for dinner. She's got her back towards me and she's moving up and down, up and down, not wearing a stitch. I stand there, gawking dumb. Her back looks like one of those lions you see on National Geographic shows, carved out and smooth. The muscles twitch and twitch back again when she moves, up down, up down, over and over.

I keep looking.

I hear something behind me and jump back, startled and embarrassed. You're not supposed to watch this part. But there's nothing there. Some trick of the wind or maybe just my guilt creeping up, tapping me on the shoulder. I sneak around the front of the house, shamey, tip-toeing my way through the gleaming frogs and fishponds. The front door is wide open, knocking around in the breeze. I hustle into the kitchen and dry myself off with a dishtowel, too scared and frinkled to go anywhere else. The kitchen is yellow linoleum and quiet, like the eye of the storm. You'd never guess what's going on in the other room. I sit down at the table and lay my head on the checkered plastic tablecloth.

I miss my room. I miss my bed. I miss being a little punk with no care in the world, giving two fucks about it, just looking for trouble.

I guess I found it.

There's a darkness here. There's something you can't put your finger on that's creeping in through the edges of the linoleum and the squares between the tiles. It's something sideways behind the drywall, something dirty and bored and mean.

I want to go home. I want my mama. All this time I thought she and I were just pure hatred. And maybe that's true a little. But maybe a little part of her looks at me and remembers about being young and now I get to be and she's not. Not no more. She traded in her young part to give me mine. I'm this red flag walking around, jarring her into the realization of all the years and all the mistakes and all the could have beens. I'm this constant reminder that she had two babies and only one got to stay.

Lord above, I wish you could have seen her. When she was young, she was like Doris Day, only sexy. She had white hair that flipped up and frosted pink lipstick and white patent-leather boots. She was the only girl in the state of Nebraska, I guarantee, that had the guts to wear knee-high shiny white boots. I have a picture of her in my head, wearing those boots, sitting on a plaid sofa, in a little pale frosty-blue mini-dress. She's holding a baby up to her shoulder and smiling at the camera.

But there's something in her smile, some giveaway behind the eyes, something scared, uncomfortable, suffering. And I wonder if that look, that far-off, buried, nervous secret, is because that baby in her arms, that baby that was me, came just a little too soon. Too quick and out of nowhere. Like one day she had hopes and dreams and then the next they were all just shut down, closed for business. When you see that look in her eyes, that sad disappointment buried deep beneath her smile, it can break your heart. The only thing that could break your heart more would be to be the reason for it.

And I wish she wouldn't have traded her life for me.

See, you never think of your parents as people. You just think of them as the gods who raised you up and poured milk in your corn-flakes. They're just the ones you always looked up to, the ones you remember always being around, fixing things, holding your hand, making a fuss about don't do this and don't do that and look both ways before your cross the street. But you never think of them as someone like you. You never think of them as some human-type person like yourself who fucks up and feels bad and gets pregnant and trades their life for you. You don't think of them like that.

I wonder if I was worth it.

I wonder how many times she wishes that baby boy had made it and not me.

Eddie comes in the kitchen and leans against the fridge. I turn my head the other way and pretend to inspect the wallpaper, little horses and cowboys riding.

"You wanna go for a drive?"

"No."

We don't look at each other. He stares at the floor and I stare at the wallpaper cowboys. There's one in the middle with blond hair, bucking high off his horse with his hat in the air. If I could just jump in, I would ride off into the sunset on the back of his saddle, into the paper horizon.

"You know how to drive?"

"No."

"You wanna learn?"

"I don't know."

"I'll teach ya."

I look over at him, suspicious of this nice-guy bent. I don't trust him as far as I could throw him, but he's playing kind. He looks up at me, slumped against the fridge, sad and leaning.

"Really?"

He nods, setting the tequila down on the counter and motioning towards the door with his head before taking his exit.

I look at the paper cowboys and the bucking broncos and, off in the distance, a cactus set down before an orange paper sun.

I follow.

I could never turn away from a car crash.

TWENTY-ONE

Jackson is a place for rich people. It's a place where the rich people are so rich, they pretend to be poor. They ignore us, noses up, as we stop at the light off Main Street. They look ahead and pretend we don't exist. They saunter around the rickety walkways and Wild West overhangs making everything look old-timey and fake. We're in the town square, the epicenter of the Old West put-on. The rich people promenade around, wearing shorts and sandals, licking ice-cream cones and looking in the shop windows, anxious to spend. Eddie parks in front of the Million-Dollar Cowboy Bar and tells me to wait in the truck. He grabs his Stetson, slams the door and strolls into the darkness.

I wait in the car for about five minutes before deciding that I'd rather go into the bar and piss off Eddie than stay out here and die of boredom. I've been hearing bits and pieces of conversation from the sidewalk: Who's dating who, Should I have bought that bag, Uncle Ted bought a boat. There's a kind of ease to it. Comfort.

People are different here. Beige. The women wear knee-length skirts and flat shoes. The men wear brand-new cowboy hats and don't swagger.

Two pale ladies in hats come strolling by. One of them stops to adjust her purse. I guess with so many bags of new-bought stuff to contend with, it's hard to get it all straight. They chatter on like two birds on a wire about Jenny and the ungodly wake-up hour for the swim team. They think it's too early. I get sick of listening to the trials and tribulations of whether or not Jenny should've joined the swim team and decide to go in. I open the door and sweep past them, but they can't be bothered to notice. I mean, not with Jenny having to wake up at five on a Saturday and all.

I walk in and it's like I just walked into a commercial for forest fires. Everything inside is made of logs, with fake branches and trees like a woodland retreat. I guess rich people like to put the outside inside. There are no seats at the bar, just saddles, one after the other. Sitting on a regular-style barstool is not an option. I take a saddle near Eddie, playing pool by himself. Behind him in a glass case is a stuffed bear, eight feet tall, his mouth froze open and his claws ready to swipe. It looks like if Eddie just took one step back, it'd all be over.

He looks at me, annoyed.

"Thought I told you to wait in the car."

"You gonna teach me to drive or what?"

The bartender takes a keen interest, stopping what he's doing to observe our mismatch. He's a plump man, pink like a pig. He's wearing a dapper new-looking denim shirt, pressed and ironed. Looks like his jeans are ironed, too.

"Not now. Not since you disobeyed a direct order."

The bartender chimes in, uneasy with Eddie seeming too much like the real thing in a town full of Disneyland cowboys.

"Hey, Mister. She can't be here," he says, drying a glass.

"Sure she can." Eddie shoots. "I can take my niece wherever I want, can't I, Luli?"

He winks, sly, as the seven ball drops in the corner pocket. I don't answer.

"That true, Missy? That your uncle?"

I look up. Eddie aims for the five ball, leaning in. There's a stale smoke hanging over us, sinking into the floorboards. Eddie hovers over the table, waiting for my answer, pretending to set up his shot.

"I guess, sir."

"You guess?"

"Yup."

"Well, then, I guess you should be leaving"

Eddie freezes mid-shot. I can tell there's gonna be trouble. Something in the arch of Eddie's crooked back makes me know that the next step is gonna be a step down and out. The next step is gonna prove we're too poor and ignorant to be mixing with dignified folk.

"Um, Eddie, maybe we should go back to Lloyd's?"

The bartender perks up at the sound of the name.

"Lloyd? Lloyd Nash?"

"Yup."

"You two friends of Lloyd's?"

"Friends," Eddie sinks the five ball, "is an understatement."

"He said Eddie's like a son to him," I blurt out, sounding shrill and desperate.

"That so?" The bartender starts to look nervous.

"Yup." Eddie sinks the three ball, leaving only the eight ball left.

"Well, um . . . hell! Friend of Lloyd's is a friend of mine. You wanna drink?" He holds up a bottle of Seagram's 7.

"Don't mind if I do." Eddie sinks the eight ball, playing it off, casual.

"Well, well, that's some pretty sharp shooting." The voice comes from the front of the bar, some newcomer just snuck in from the sun.

To say the newcomer is an ugly man is putting it nice. Real nice. He's got a face that'd make a freight train take a dirt road. He's got faded everything, not just-bought, like the rest of the town, with gray stubble peppering the bottom of his face and a tooth missing, smack-dab in front. He takes a seat, sideways, leaning against the saddle, looking gritty down the bar.

And now he is looking at me.

"Well, it's hotter then a French whore with two pussies out there, huh?"

He unbuttons his collar.

Look, I'm not trying to say I'm some kinda beauty queen or princess priss from Prissonia, but the way he's looking at me, it's like he wants to eat me up right there. And there's something in his look that's making me nervous and shamey and weak, like my knees are about to wobble out from underneath me. Eddie comes over and stands beside me, protective. I like this new side of Eddie, like I'm his girlfriend.

"I like your hat," the stranger says, making nice.

"It's not a hat. It's a Stetson."

"Well, then, I like your Stetson."

"You play?" Eddie nods towards the pool table.

"I reckon I can, been a while but—"

"You a betting man?"

The bartender hands Eddie a drink, eyeing the stranger, wary.

"All right. Let's make it a hundred."

The stranger starts to smile crooked, meeting Eddie in the eye.

"Well, well. All right. You're on, then."

The bartender and I share a look, both of us thinking that this is how all the bad things in the world begin and that there is no doubt these two are the men for the job. The bartender pours me a drink.

"Shirley Temple, kid. Made it special, just for you."

"Thanks, Mister."

He leans in, dimming his voice to a whisper,

"Listen, kid, we don't want any trouble here, so, you know, if things start looking bad, maybe you could call off your uncle there and tell him you wanna go back to Lloyd's."

I nod back, assuring, squinting my eyes like we have an agreement, man to man.

Eddie racks up the balls, giving it a little flourish at the end to show he means business. The stranger fumbles with the pool cue.

I sip my Shirley Temple and try to act casual, but how can you when Eddie shoots in every single ball, each one after the next, missing the eight, on purpose.

The stranger looks flustered, disappointed. He goes to the table, his only chance a solid damn near the side pocket. Tough shot. He misses off the bank. Eddie shoots in the eight ball and starts to laugh.

"Well, there, Mister, now maybe you'll learn some manners."

The stranger looks sunken, shaking his head and scratching his neck, stubbly.

"You got me, Mister."

"Well, live and learn, I guess." Eddie's being a real pal now.

"Listen." The stranger leans in to Eddie, quiet-like. "I can't go back to my wife a hundred bucks in the hole. She'll have my head, if you know what I mean."

The stranger looks up at Eddie, pleading. "Maybe we could play one more, you know, double or nothing."

Eddie looks at the man like he just landed off the moon.

"You must be one dumb crazy fucker to wanna lose two-hundred bucks."

"All right, then. How bout a game for two-hundred straight up? That worth your time?"

The bartender and I share a look. This is just too pathetic.

The stranger looks at Eddie.

"Could be."

Eddie walks over to the table and starts chalking up his cue.

The stranger and Eddie shoot to see who goes first. The stranger wins. Eddie comes over and stands beside me at the bar, drinking his drink and watching the man, pathetic in his stance. The stranger makes the first shot. Eddie nods, not thinking much of it. The stranger makes the second shot. Eddie shifts his weight and sips his drink. The stranger makes the third shot, the fourth shot, the fifth shot, all the way to the end when he sinks the eight ball, like it's nothing much to write home about.

I look up at the bartender, helpless. The bartender shrugs.

Eddie stands there, still, blood boiling underneath.

The stranger meets his gaze, blank, but somewhere behind his eyes there's a sneer and a twinkling, born bad. He's proved Eddie's untrue grit.

"I believe you owe me a hundred dollars. I'll take cash, thank you."

Eddie stares at the man, sizing him up.

"I'm not paying."

"What? I didn't hear you?"

"I'm not paying."

"Oh, okay, well then, in that case . . . I'll make you a deal."

The stranger comes up close to Eddie and starts whispering in his ear, looking over, here and there. I catch his eye quick and he looks away, guilty. Eddie listens and listens, asks him a question and listens some more. The bartender wipes off the counter, trying to make-pretend he's part of the wall. I'm the only one who senses something bubbling, something filthy and unkind.

Eddie comes sidling over, leaning his elbow on the bar, putting his hand on my shoulder, nice.

"Now, Luli, we got man stuff to discuss now, so I want you to just go back there and wait a spell."

"Back where?"

"Back there." He nods toward the bathroom, quick.

"Nuh-uh, no way."

"Luli, look, I'm in trouble here, all right, and I need you to help me, can you do that? Can you help me?"

I hesitate, looking to the floor for an answer.

"C'mon, darlin . . . you like that? You like that when I call you darlin?"

He picks up my chin now and starts talking quiet.

"I think you do. I think you like it a lot. I bet there's some other things you'd like, too. Am I right?"

I bite my lip and nod, barely. I can't stand it. This is a special bar trick I know by heart. He's writing the lines now. Somehow this got turned round and he's writing the lines. I just want him to call me girlfriend names and make nice and pull my chin up. I just want him to stay like this, protective.

"I guess."

"You guess. Well, okay, then, just go back there and wait a spell while we talk business, quick, and then we'll go for a nice drive, maybe get some ice cream."

Something doesn't add up. Something doesn't add up and I'm letting it not add up and I don't know why. There's something pulling me, shifting back and forth.

Here are the gears. There's this one about getting called sweet names. There goes that one about learning how to drive and a fantasy date with an ice cream cone. There's this other one about some sneaky bet off to the side. There's this one, too, about naysaying. Then there's this one, this lumbering gear, about wanting to ride off into the sunset with Eddie, treating me nice. Can you hear them shifting? Can you hear them shifting back and forth, back and forth, jamming up, getting loose, shifting forward, shifting back and getting stuck all over again?

TWENTY-TWO

The bathroom in the Million-Dollar Cowboy Bar is more like a few bucks. There's a light buzzing overhead, trapping a few dead bugs, in silhouette squares on the ceiling. The room seems painted green until, upon closer inspection, you realize there's actually not one bit of green in it at all, but the light above bathing everything white into fishy.

In the mirror, my face looks spooky and worn down, like some kind of broken-down ghost, left over November 1st. I've been waiting here for about three minutes, crunching gears, and I don't know what I'm waiting for, but I know it's not good.

There's a squeaking and a shifting and, finally, a lock into place and next thing I know I'm heading out the door because this math just does not add up and I write these lines, this is my show. But before I get there, the door opens and I find myself face to face with the ugly stranger. He stands there looking at me like a wolf looks at a sheep. He's got a long nose, stretching too far down, almost to his lip, skinny. I decide to put my head back on my shoulders and get this thing squared away.

"Let me by, Mister."

He stays put, blocking my way, staring.

"Why don't you take a picture, it'll last longer," I say, leaning against the sink, trying to act casual. If he won't let me by straight, maybe I can sidle through sideways.

"I wish I could, believe me. I wish I could."

He starts to come closer and I stand my ground, not wanting to seem scared. You got to treat lowlifes like horses, if they smell fear, they know they got the upper hand. I'm wondering when Eddie is gonna interrupt this little romance but I have a feeling, a broken-down kind of feeling, that this one is on me. The light flickers above us and if this man looked bad standing in the dim light of the bar, in the green fluorescent he looks like twenty miles of country road. I can't believe it but he's starting to salivate. This I've never seen before, so I'm real-quick lost in a strange fascination with the spit building up on the sides of his lip. I got to get out.

"Well, Mister, it's been nice meeting you and all, but—"

"You ain't going nowhere."

"Oh yeah, keep dreaming."

And with that I march right on past him, straight for the door. My plan works perfect except that he grabs me by the hair and pulls me back towards him, whispering in my ear, "I haven't got my hundred bucks' worth."

I think I can actually hear my heart cracking into bits and pieces, falling clink clink clink down the green sink drain. I muster up the courage, trying to get my soul back out the sink, and ask, "What are you getting at, Mister?"

"You're the bet, little girl. Your uncle lost."

"What? What the hell is that supposed to mean? Where's Eddie?"

"You've been traded."

He chuckles, pulling my arms behind my back and swinging me into the nearest stall. I struggle against him, squirming in and out of his reach, lashing out, but it's no good. For a skinny little fucker he can fight. He forces my head back into the metal stall, cupping his hand over my mouth. I bite. He cackles out, pleased.

"I see we got a live one here."

He grabs my wrists with his other hand and lifts them back behind my head. I am waiting for Eddie and sinking into the realization he's not coming. I am squirming and fighting and clawing and squirming, but he's wearing me down. He and his breath and his skinny long nose and his gritty teeth and his gray stubble chin. Each little outburst is leaving me more and more exhausted, panting, trying again, panting again. He's stronger than me and it's not a fair fight. But we all know about fair in this life. That's something for movies with courtrooms.

I go to kick him between the legs but he blocks me. He stops my leg with his knee and then forces my legs apart with his body. He's holding me down now, pressed up against me. He's looking directly into my eyes, not two inches away, like he's getting off on how much I hate him. You may think this is the part where I'm supposed to cry, but I ain't letting that happen. No sir. He ain't getting that outta me. He leans in closer and whispers into my ear, "You know what I like to do to little girls like you?"

I look at him, waiting for his answer, about as defiant as a girl can be with her mouth gagged, her arms pinned and her legs spread wide open by a toothless stranger.

"I like to break em in."

He smiles a derelict little smile and traces his tongue on my neck. He bites the bottom of my shirt and pulls it up with his teeth, keeping me gagged and pinned. He starts working his way all around my neck and chest with his mouth, looking up at me like I'm supposed to like it, grinning a degenerate grin like this is his Christmas. He starts concentrating on the pink part of my chest.

And this is where the strange thing happens. This is where the thing that's not supposed to happen, that no one ever talks about, happens. There must be something wrong with me, some screw loose in the back of my head, because even though this is a sick old dirty old toothless old man, ugly as the day he was born . . .

I start to like it.

There's something going on, new and tingly, that is somehow on the other side of justice and reason and everything my mama told me about what you should and should not do. I know now that I am a wrong dirty girl, the kind that ends up sleeping in an alley somewhere by the truck stop and waiting for the next batch of truckers to come in. I am the kind of girl who ought to be ashamed and curse herself and not worth living. And I am, I am ashamed of myself, right here, in this moment, blushing and sweating and feeling about five thousand different things at once. I know, in this moment, that I am my mama's daughter and that I am rotten to the core.

And I think there's something to my flushing or my shortness of breath, because this sweaty old drunk, pinning me down, takes a moment, stops for a moment and looks at me, real deep breathing, like he's seeing the back of my head. And he catches me and he reads my mind and he, slow and mean, breaks into an ugly little satisfied grin. And in this moment, this moment that feels like a dare, the door slams open and there he is, fucking finally, Eddie.

He flattens the stranger, grabs me out the stall and pushes me through the back door of the Million-Dollar Cowboy Bar, hurling me into the cab of the truck.

He rushes around, gets in the driver's seat and takes off, looking back like he's worried our little degenerate is gonna round up a posse to collect on his bet. But I know he's not. He's not.

He got what he wanted.

TWENTY-THREE

Just cause you're a loser don't give you the right to sell me off like some two-bit hooker."

I don't tell him the shamey part. I don't tell him about the part when I started to turn into all the bad things you're not supposed to be.

Part of me is thinking that this fucker sitting next to me is some kind of knight in shining armor come to rescue me from a green bathroom but the other part is thinking, Well, if it wasn't for him, I wouldn't have been pinned down there in the first place.

And I wonder if this is the way love goes. You put some fella on a pedestal and then little by little they chip away at that little personal fantasy, chink by chink, until one day you realize they're just a regular old shitbag like the rest. But by then, you've been workin so hard to keep the dream alive that you're not about to chuck the whole thing altogether, like you're just sticking around cause you're too stubborn to admit you made a mistake.

I'd bet twelve bucks that's what happened to my mama. One day she just looked at my dad and thought, "What the fuck did I settle for you for?" Can't say I blame her, trying to raise up one kid on nothin but Saltines and Halloween candy, after losing the other one. You might just start fucking the neighbor yourself.

"What? You think I sold you off?"

"Uh. Yeah."

"Well, you're wrong, Luli, you're just plain wrong about that."

"Yeah, right, listen, I wasn't born yesterday so you can just—"

"Look, that was all part of my plan."

"Oh, this is gonna be good."

"It was, see, I was just buying time, is all."

"Yeah, right, you must have me confused with some Okie if you think I'm trying to buy that song and dance."

"There are a lot of nice people from Oklahoma, Luli."

"What?"

"I said there's a lot of nice people from Oklahoma that probably wouldn't like it if they heard you say what you just said . . . about being an Okie."

"What the fuck are you talking about? You just threw me in a shitbar bathroom with some gap-toothed retard and you're talking to me about manners?"

"Retard is also not a very nice thing to call someone."

"Oh my Lord. You are bonkers. You really are."

"I'm just saying."

"Let me out."

"Look, Luli, you ever stop to think that maybe you don't know everything? You ever stop to think that maybe someone twice your age might maybe know a little more about getting out of a hundred? Huh? It's called strategy."

"Hmph. Wull, maybe next time you ought to run it by me first, how bout that?"

"Well, maybe next time you'll stick in the truck like I said."

We pull up to a creamy peach ice cream stand with a sign from the Fifties. There's a charcoal little patch of a parking lot with a family of four standing in front of the window going back and forth about sundaes and maybe sprinkles and vanilla or chocolate or what about a banana split. All four of them are wearing shorts with fat pink ankles coming down like they've been eating ice cream for three weeks straight. There's no fence or anything between the rickety stand and the wide open plain behind it, heading off into the Tetons and the sun burning down, turning ankles red and melting ice cream off the cone.

They're so caught up in the complexities of sprinkles and syrup and how much is too much and how much is not enough and maybe a Diet Coke, too, that they don't even see us, engine idling, behind. If Eddie thinks some dumb ice cream cone is gonna wipe this pout off my face he's got another thing coming, that's for sure.

"You can get out, Luli, but then you don't get an ice cream."

"I don't want a dumb ice cream. I don't even like ice cream."

"C'mon, Luli, everybody likes ice cream."

"No, they don't. I don't. Ergo. Not everybody likes ice cream."

"Ergo?"

"Yeah. Ergo. Therefore. Hence."

"Where you learn all that?"

"My World Book Encyclopedia, thank you very much."

"Well, next time look up strategy."

"Tsh. My middle name is strategy."

"Oh, well, then, you must be smart. Smart and pretty, that's a deadly combination."

"Hmph."

"Deadly."

"You think I'm pretty?"

"Guess."

"Wull, do you or don't you?"

"I think if it wasn't for that horrible mouth of yours . . . some people, not me, of course, but some people might find you kinda somewhat attractive . . . in a furry little animal sort of way."

The family of four waddles past us, stacked full, over to the plastic picnic bench, white and cream, taking too long adjusting, readjusting, big arms and legs, in and around the too-small bench. I guess people got fatter somewhere between then and now, or that bench shrunk, either way. They're content, though, now that they got their banana split and their sundae and vanilla soft-serve swirl. You can lap up sprinkles and look up at the mountains and never think once to maybe venture up. You can sip a Diet Coke and talk about the weather if you have to talk about anything but why bother when you've got that fancy vanilla swirl spelling out happiness in a sugar cone.

"This whole fucking country is going to the dogs."

We sit and watch the lappers lapping.

"It's changing, Luli, it's changing, and once it's gone, it's gone."

He takes off his hat and squints at the brim. I wish you could see the bright blue sky behind him and the sun beating down and hear the movie music start to play. I have been looking for my leading man since my dad walked off the set in Palmyra, and, ladies and gentlemen, I have found him. He's an Elvis-style cowboy with complicated ideas about how the West was lost, how the country was bought and sold, how the calf was fattened. You can't see it now, but let me put him in hair and make-up and dust him off and shine the light. Let me set him up top of a white patch horse and cue the music and you just wait, you just wait, you'll see it then, you'll see it then.

He can ride up to the tippy-top of the wedding cake and I will meet him, I will meet him, I will climb up, tier by tier, and meet him smack-dab on top of the fifth layer of frosting and he'll dip his Stetson and call me sweetheart and darlin and sugar-pie and you may not see it yet, but believe me, just wait, it'll hit you like a ton of bricks.

"You want some ice cream or what?"

We stare at the lappers and the creamy shack, the gold Tetons in the distance, pulling up towards the sun.

"Nope."

"Me neither."

He guns the engine back and next thing you know it's just him and me on the two-lane blacktop and I have a feeling that at any moment the wheels of the truck are gonna fly off the pavement and we're gonna drive off into the clouds and leave this whole vanilla swirl carnival behind, pop bang swoosh, and into the big blue sky.

TWENTY-FOUR

We pull up to a run-down old shack, hidden behind some trees and a gutted white Impala, sitting there in the front like it's gunning to take off.

"I thought you said you were gonna take me driving."

Eddie cuts the engine and gets out, "We're driving, ain't we?"

"No, but I thought you said you were gonna teach me."

"I am. Just gotta run some errands first. Real quick."

He winks and walks towards the screen door, barely hanging off the hinge. I stick to my guns in the truck.

"Ya coming?"

"No."

"Suit yourself." He shrugs and walks in.

I sit there staring at the shack, some shade of ancient aqua faded down to gray, chipping off the sides. The whole thing is leaning off in one direction, like it's fixing to run south, just waiting for its shot.

Eddie peeks his head out.

"Look, you might as well just come inside. I got some friends I want you to meet."

"Whatta you care?"

"Well, it looks weird, you just sitting out here and all."

"So."

"Well, I think it's rude."

I don't want nothing more to do with him and his stupid bets and his whiskey smoke drinking all night long and who cares anyways.

"Don't you wanna be nice?"

He gives me a look like I ought to know better and I think back to what my dad said on the stairs about how a girl's supposed to be sweet, don't get mean.

Well, what am I gonna do, sit in the truck all afternoon?

I get up, follow him inside and right away I get it.

There's two girls, actually, girls is stretching it, how bout women dressed like girls, sitting on the bed. The bed is in the front room and they are perched there in their miniskirts like they've been there for weeks. Both of them are wearing tube tops, one pink, the other white-and-black stripes. Both of them are wearing plastic chunky heels and they look like they've been up for five years straight. One of them has short dark hair like a boy and the other has short red hair like a boy. They look like matching salt and pepper shakers.

But the thing that you get the most off them, the thing that just drips off the bed and into the room, is that they've seen it all and don't care about any of it anymore.

They look up at me when I walk in and one of them looks at the other like they're in cahoots. The other one looks at Eddie.

"Who's the jailbait?"

"She's my niece."

"Yeah, right."

Eddie throws some money on the bed and the brunette grabs it, counting it out. She goes into the back room and the redhead looks up at Eddie, her upper lip swirling up into a smile.

"Aren't you gonna introduce us?"

"Luli, this is Sherri. Sherri, this is Luli."

"Nice to meet you, Luli. So how long have you been Eddie's, uh, niece?"

"Um."

I look up, expecting to see her poised for an answer, but instead she's leaning over her knees, like a C in a mini-skirt, itching her ankles. She's scratching like a stray cat and I look closer at the red dime-size sores decorating her shins down to her feet. Some of them are open and bleeding but she keeps scratching and trying not to scratch and scratching again.

The brunette comes back in and throws Eddie a Ziploc bag full of white powder.

"Nearly cleaned me out."

Eddie tucks the bag away under his shirt and sits down.

"Luli, this is Crystal."

Crystal looks over and gives me an amused nod.

I look down at the floor, inspecting the wine-colored rug, full of dust and dog hair and ashes seeped in. There's a joke in the air, a little source of entertainment to the girls that I think might just be me. I try to wonder if it's my face or my clothes or just my sheer existence that's turning these girls into silent giggling and sideways glances. Sherri stops scratching and then starts again. Stop. Start.

Stop. Start. It's a busy little movement, frantic, desperate, that the three of us not on the bed are pretending to ignore.

On the other side of the room, Crystal leans against the wallpaper, burgundy and cream, like something regal peeling off. In her tank top and little skirt and short boy haircut, it's like she's got a whole different concept of what's supposed to reel them in. She leans over, lights a cigarette and gives Eddie a nod.

"You wanna hit that?"

Eddie shrugs, takes the baggie out and throws it on the bed. I excuse myself and go to the bathroom to express my disgust. On my way out I give Eddie a look like he better fucking hurry his ass cause I don't have all day to sit around with a bunch of bimbos snorting speed and scratching ankles.

The bathroom is tiny with pink tile, pink paint, pink bathtub and a pink shower curtain. There's glitter and lip gloss and Aqua-Net and diapers and that's what throws me off. I splash my face and wonder if Glenda's worried about me. I tip-toe out into the room in between and there it is, sitting off to the side underneath the window, a little yellow crib. I sidle over and peer in and am surprised, no, shocked, no, disappointed, no, worried to see this little tiny baby just laying there, sleeping soft, like it don't know it got shit for a life yet.

I stand there, looking down at this little fragile thing and wondering what the hell this world has come to and thanking my lucky stars that my mama at least had the good sense to get a husband and a house with two floors.

But then I remember something, something dark and churning that I made myself forget back when I had little arms and little legs and my mama had a blue dress. I remember something and I would keep remembering, I sure would, if it wouldn't make my heart fall out my chest and stop the earth from turning.

I can't think about that. I can't think about that part now.

I look around the floor beneath me and there's nothing but clothes and make-up and shoes stacked on top of shoes, each one higher than the next. There's a half-eaten pizza sitting in an open box on the table in the corner covered in what I think are olives, from first glance, and this is the part that makes you want to cover your mouth, cause those aren't olives. Those are cockroaches, count em, six of em, having what must seem like a feast in their meager vermin existence.

I start to back out.

In the other room I can hear Sherri going on to Crystal about how she's gonna take a pottery class and that she's sick of this town and that it's really time for her to get her act together and that she's really gonna do it this time. Crystal keeps saying uh-huh, uh-huh and adding that she's gonna go with her, maybe they could take the pottery class together. Maybe they could start a pottery store back in Jackson, cause that's what rich folks like to buy and together they could design the store and they could make a fortune and they're gonna do it soon, next month even, no, wait, has to be next year cause Crystal has that thing over Christmas, well, maybe in the spring then, but soon, anyway, real soon.

Eddie is listening, smoking a cigarette and gnashing his teeth. I come out of the room, the room with the baby and the heels and the cockroaches on the pizza, look at Eddie and take a stance.

"We're leaving."

Crystal and Sherri interrupt their grand plans, look up and look at Eddie, who just sits there, teeth gnashing.

"What's the hurry?"

"The hurry is that I'm leaving and you can come or not but I ain't staying."

Sherri and Crystal look at each other like I am playing my part perfectly as the butt of their jokes. They try hard not to giggle but then Sherri can't help it and she lets out a little snort and Crystal tries to shush her up but now they both start chuckling and trying not to and chuckling harder. And ain't it just great when you can live your life so carefree and sexy and dressed up and high-heeled and who cares that you've got a baby in the back room with a pizza full of cockroaches and no hope for the future?

Eddie doesn't look at me.

I look at the girls trying not to giggle and Eddie gnashing his teeth and the shitty wine carpet and the regal crest wallpaper peeling down the wall and Sherri scratching her ankles and I walk directly out the screen door, past the truck and down the road.

And as I'm marching off into the setting sun it starts to dawn on me that maybe my mama didn't fuck up completely because if she had then maybe I would have been raised up in some room with flea-bite ankles and cockroach pizza in a house leaning over into the abyss. And maybe I am just a two-bit hick from the heartland but I do know one thing, my mama did not raise me to be skankin it in skanksville with the skanks.

TWENTY-FIVE

I get about three and a half telephone poles down the road before Eddie pulls up, smiling like he just won the lottery, acting like James Dean on crack. I have had enough and I am walking without looking sideways, straight ahead, and I don't care if I never see him again and get left out here in the middle of crap county just as long as Eddie's out the picture for good. But now he's driving three miles an hour beside me, yelling over the motor through the passenger-side window, not even bothering to look at the road.

"C'mon, kid, I told you I had errands."

"Keep driving."

"Well, fine but I thought you might wanna know that Glenda called and was asking about you and wanted us to meet her at the Motel 6 in Devil's Slide."

"Motel 6? Yeah, right. I don't believe you."

"Cause she said Lloyd was having a meeting and she didn't want to ruin it, what with it being business and all. She said she owed you."

"Owed me what?"

"I dunno. She just said she did."

"Hm. Sounds weird."

"Well, look, she said to be there. You can come or not, but, if you don't, she's gonna take it out on me, so you can see my dilemma."

I stop in my tracks and ponder the sun setting yonder over the horizon. I'll be double fucked if I have to spend the night out here in a ditch with not even my bag for a pillow. The truck idles next to me and I take a deep breath. There's something inside me whispering whatever you do, don't get in that truck, don't get in that truck, don't get in that truck, but I am kicking myself knowing that in just a split second I am gonna sigh and throw my hands up in the air and get right back in that truck.

Eddie doesn't look at me as we scratch out onto the road towards Devil's Slide. He doesn't look at me and he doesn't say one word about Glenda or what she owes me.

TWENTY-SIX

I guess you could say my feelings towards Eddie are balanced somewhere between fear and want. There's a feeling I have, when I look at him, that he's about to vanish before my very eyes, like some magic cowboy trick conjured up to scare me but keep me on the edge of my seat. And I am. I cannot get off my toes for a minute for fear that he'll be gone for good and I'll be an all-alone girl. It's that feeling of impending abandonment that keeps me clinging to him like he's the last train out of crapville.

He's an ugly man. No doubt about it. He's crooked on the inside and on the out, like his mind warbled in on itself and his body just followed suit. But there's something in his eyes, something rough and cunning, that keeps me from opening that truck door, tumbling out onto the gravel and running back to Jackson.

There's a wish I have, when I close my eyes. I pray that he'll fall for me. And it's just cause I know he won't that I want this so bad. There are no spells I can cast, no webs I can weave, no magic words and candles burned. It's like he can see right through me, straight to the core and has it on fact that I ain't worth it.

Two miles outside Devil's Slide, we pull into the Motel 6. Not my dream date. I twiddle my thumbs in the car while Eddie checks us into the furthest room from the road. I look around for Glenda's car but I guess she's not here yet. Makes sense, she had farther to drive and maybe got a late start. The moon hangs silver in the sky, waning. There's a few stars turning on, one by one, but mostly they're just getting warmed up.

We walk into number 12 and it's like the room is made of cork. There's a silence while the two of us stare at the double bed, made crisp.

"That's all they had, kid, don't complain."

"All right." I nod. "But how's Glenda gonna find us?"

"Don't worry bout it."

"Wull, should we leave a message?"

"Already did."

He turns on the TV and some long-haired man with a tan starts screaming at us, from the box, telling us we better not miss out on the last chance to buy his brand new-fangled exerciser. Eddie lays down on the bed and starts flipping through the channels, all the way through and then back again, all the way through and then back again. He settles on the crime channel, talking about some lady found on her kitchen linoleum, half-rotten, her dogs and cats, flea-infested, pissing and shitting all over the floor, and this is the part where the nice-looking cop gets choked up and quiet, real concerned, telling us about how the dogs and cats were feeding off her corpse. That's how he put it. Feeding.

Eddie makes a face and grabs a bottle of Jack Daniels out the sack by the side of the bed. He's a long man. His legs go from one end of the bed to the other, one folded on top, not even straight out. He starts switching channels. Switch. Wait. Switch. Wait. Switch.

I go to take a shower, wanting to get the old geezer and the cockroach pizza and the dog-and-cat-eaten lady off me and out of my skin. I take off my clothes in the steam, wondering if I look good. I don't even remember what looking good looks like. But I want to. I want Eddie to look at my shiny new body and be rendered helpless. I want him to lift my chin and call me honey.

But that's a long shot.

When I was little I used to watch Tammy play dress-up. She would twirl around in front of the mirror, looking herself up and down, quiet, contemplating with two small wrinkles furrowed into her brow. That serious squint, that need and desperation, increased ten-fold with age. The older she got, the less fancy-free dress-up became. She went from twirling to turning to standing still to frowning silent.

When I was ten, my dad and I sat at the kitchen table still while she knocked bottle after bottle of Wind Song and Shalimar and Charlie onto the floor. For her grand finale, she threw a bottle of Jean Naté at her reflection, shattering the mirror into thousands of mite-sized pieces, shining out like diamonds in the orange shag rug. My dad and I sat there, contemplating the tabletop, waiting for the show to stop.

When her number was up, she passed out on the bed and he got up, quiet, quiet going up the stairs, quiet, getting down on his knees, quiet, picking up the little mini-diamonds, one by one. Then he walked to the bathroom, threw them out, quiet, walked to the bathroom, threw them out. He wouldn't let me help, wouldn't even let me in the room, even though his hands were bleeding at all ten fingertips and even though it was an endless job that never did get done.

The next morning my mama woke up, came down the stairs and asked, "What the fuck happened to the mirror?" It was the kind of thing you would laugh at, if it wasn't your mama. My dad didn't even look up from his cornflakes. He just took the blame, said he broke it and promised to buy her a new one straightaway. She walked out into the hall, shaking her head and mumbling about what kinduva idiot husband she had who'd be so clumsy as to break a mirror, seven years' bad luck and all.

That happened when I was ten. So I reckon I got four more years in payment.

I inspect my reflection. I'm starting to look like her. My body is starting to make the same shapes her body makes, bubbling up. I don't know what it is I'm supposed to look like. I don't know what it is I'm supposed to be. With Eddie in the other room I feel off my game and peculiar, like I've done something wrong, but I don't know what. He makes me lose my courage. He makes me feel like I wish I was better or prettier or just plain not me. He makes me feel like I'll never be good enough and he's right.

"You gonna be in there all night?" he yells out over the TV.

I put my clothes back on and walk out to find him sitting on the bed in nothing but his underwear, the bottle of Jack Daniels leaning against the headrest and a make-shift drink in a see-through cup resting where his belly's supposed to be. His body is angled and disjointed like one of those paintings where the people are made up of circles and cubes. His hipbones cut through his skivvies, razor-sharp, and you can count his ribs from the front. He looks up at me.

"Jack and Coke. Cures what ails ya."

He takes a drink. "What the hell you put those dusty ol clothes back on for?"

"Cause I don't have nothin else."

I try to position myself out from under the green fluorescent light. None too flattering. "It's not my fault you decided to drive off into the sunset."

But Eddie's back to flipping channels. My head could catch fire and he wouldn't notice.

"When's Glenda supposed to get here?"

He ignores me. Switch. Wait. Switch. Wait. Switch.

"Eddie, when is Glenda supposed to get here?"

Nothing.

"Hello?"

Eddie hits the mute and lets out a huff.

"Well, that's the thing, kid, there's something I wanted to talk to you about."

And I know right then and there that I am never gonna see Glenda again.

"You see, me and Glenda had a talk, well, actually, she came to me first and . . . well, she asked me if, well, she asked me . . . to take you."

I am trying not to hear what he's saying. I am trying to pretend that it's a few minutes before. I am trying to make it come out different.

"Whattaya mean, take me? Take me where?"

"I don't know, wherever, she just said she couldn't keep you around, cause of Lloyd and all, and that she wanted me to take you . . . off her hands." He shrugs. "Sorry."

"I don't believe you. She wouldn't do that."

"Oh yes she would. She would and she did. Look, she even gave me a grand to take care of you."

Eddie takes out a wad of bills from the bag next to the bed, showing it to me. It's the other wad of bills from Custer's Last Stand. Her half. "She said she felt bad but that she wanted me to take care of you, make sure you stay out of trouble."

I am looking at myself in the middle of this cork-pile room, wood-paneled and cubby-holed, in the middle of this Motel 6, two miles outside Devil's Slide, Utah, and realizing that this is it. This is all there is for me.

"Look, kid, I know you think I'm some kinda freak and Glenda is little Miss Perfect, but let me tell you something, she's trouble and you're better off without her. Besides, I ain't so bad. I don't bite."

And I am watching him swigging his Jack Daniels, getting surly and meaner with each swig, till I can see something else, something that does bite, cueing up behind his eyes, some demon sent from drunkville to drown the Devil's Slide Motel 6.

I am not sticking around for the show.

"You know, maybe I ought to get some ice."

He's burning a hole into the carpet, forest green, turning brown around the edges.

"Want anything?"

"Huh?"

"You want anything, you know, like some Fritos or something?"

"Did I say I wanted anything?"

"No."

"Wull, then, I guess I don't, then, do I?"

He's getting to that mean part of the drunk show. Drink number four or five.

It's gonna get worse before it gets better. I guess he left the romantic part back in Jackson. I guess he left that part for the day.

Maybe if he ate something he might just get grumpy mean but not mean mean, like the kind that does that Dr. Jekyll and Mr. Hyde thing where you're watching a person and they get that faraway staring look in their eyes and, around drink number six, transform into someone else, some dark version of themselves sent from a parallel universe where everything you say is wrong and you're gonna get a beating for sure, so you might as well buck up and stop trying.

I walk out, slamming the door behind me. I do not want to stick around for drink number seven or eight through nine.

We're on the second floor and you have to walk on the outside balcony, past all the rooms, to get anywhere. The floor is covered in Astro-turf, wet and worn, like there's a pool somewhere nearby. I wander around, looking for the ice machine, ending up in a dead end and then another dead end and then one more.

It's misty out here, quiet. There's an eerie buzz underneath everything, like there's a plug buried deep beneath the hotel that you could just pull out and the whole place would vanish into thin air, never to be seen again. I'm beginning to think I just stepped into some late-night fluorescent Astro-turf mirage, some spaceship version of reality, going nowhere fast, walking around in circles in some made-up maze with aliens watching for their own personal amusement. And then another dead end.

I give up on the upstairs and decide to venture down to the first floor. There's a light coming from somewhere down there, with voices echoing off the white plaster walls. I walk towards the action and find myself staring at three high school jocks playing Marco Polo in a chintzy pool.

One by one, they look up at me, unconscious, stopping their game. There's no way to play this off. They're staring at me and I'm staring at them, plain and simple. Seems like the rest of the world just dropped off the face of the earth.

"Hi," I squeak out, sounding more like a lizard than a real live girl, with dreams and a newfound body to get them with.

The boys look at each other, silent, deciding who's gonna talk first or if they should even bother to answer at all. Nothing.

I give up, chalking it up to them being rich and me being some country-fried lowlife from the sticks. I spot the ice machine over in the vending area on the other side of the pool and give it a go, wishing I didn't have to walk past their perfect-life stares.

One of the boys gets out of the pool and walks towards me. He's dripping wet and coming closer.

I'm too shy to look at him, so I put all my attention into the ice machine, burying my head deep inside, pretending to use all my concentration to scoop out the ice with the scooper.

"Careful. That thing might swallow you up."

"Ha ha, funny," I say, before I can stop myself. Being a smart-aleck is second nature.

He unhooks the little swinging door above me, threatening to drop it on my head.

"Tell me your name or you'll be sorry."

He smiles down at me, holding the chrome door so it teeters perilous over my head. Looking up at him for the first time, I notice that he is about sixteen and much too good-looking to be talking to me. He's spoiled-looking and handsome, with green eyes and light-brown hair, the color of ashes. He has that confidence you get from never having to worry what you're gonna eat for dinner or if there's even anything coming at all, like he's entitled to a fun life and every moment is just a part of the ongoing heaven of pleasant surprises and bouncy youth. His skin has this undertone glow of olive, like he never ate a Twinkie his whole life. He smiles at me with perfect teeth and I regret that I was ever born.

"C'mon, then, what's your name . . . you better tell me or you're gonna get it."

"Luli." Again, like a lizard.

"Come again?"

"Luli. My name's Luli."

I finish scooping the ice and stand straight, owning up. He closes the chrome door.

"Well, that's a weird name."

"Yeah, wull, it was nice meeting you."

I start to walk off, awkward. I don't fit in and never will. I'm too lowborn for them, might as well just face facts.

"Hey! Excuse me? Aren't you gonna ask my name?"

I stop in my tracks, turning slightly. I've got my feet pointed forward but my top twisted back, like a contorted pretzel trying to play it cool.

"No."

"Well, why not?"

"Because I don't care."

I start walking.

He stops and then lets out a laugh, collapsing everything back into good fun and high times. He's not gonna let this world turn bad on him, no sir.

"Okay. Well, then, I'll tell you anyway. My name's Clement."

"Oh, and you say my name's weird?"

"It's a family name."

"Oh."

The two of us stand there, sizing each other up, trying to pretend we're not. His two friends make believe they're not watching from the pool.

"You ever hear of the category game?"

"The what?"

"The category game. It's this game we like to play with cards, just face cards."

"Why's it called the category game?"

"Well, cause, if you turn over a Jack you have to think of a category."

"What kind of a category?"

"Oh, I don't know, could be anything. Like . . . things you would find in a hardware store . . . or fake rock bands, in alphabetical order. So, then, if you went first, you would say something like . . . Acid Head. And then the second person would say something like . . . Black Serpent. Or something like that. And then you just go around and around until someone can't think of anything or someone repeats . . . and then they have to drink."

"Sounds stupid."

He laughs again and looks at his friends, still pretend ignoring.

"It is stupid. That's why we play it. C'mon, you should try it. It'll be fun."

"Um. I dunno . . . I'm kind of supposed to be getting back."

"Just one game. One game. I promise. It'll be fun."

He grabs the ice outta my hand and motions to the corner, where they've got their towels set up on a cooler, hiding the beer under a table with a white-and-blue umbrella and four matching white plastic chairs.

Clement takes out a chair for me and doesn't move till I sit down. I look up at him, nervous to be treated so good. He sits across from me, smiling to his friends over his shoulder. I don't like it. I don't want to be some inside joke between friends, some girl you fiddled with in some cheap hotel in Utah.

Just then two older folks walk up and smile big, looking proud down at Clement and his two friends, still pretend playing in the pool. The man is on the tubbier side but he's got an air about him, something tan and comforting, like a dad you'd see on TV, the kind that takes his sons hunting and buys his daughter a pony for her sweet sixteen. Next to him stands a woman who looks exactly like a horse.

If you took a horse and gave it tits and a blond head of hair, that would be this woman. And that's not all. There's something about her, something conniving and cheap, like she's just along for the ride and hit the jackpot with Mr. Comfort. She wears a white vest, somewhere between a dress shirt and a tank top, with a pair of new-bought, too-tight jeans. I can't believe this woman is hanging off Mr. Comfort's elbow. If she could get this guy, with her horsemouth, then my mama, with her blond flip and steel-gray eyes, ought to be able to land a billionaire.

Clement puts his feet up on the cooler, casual.

"Luli, this is my dad, Buck."

Mr. Comfort looks at me, tan and charming. "Nice to meet you, Luli."

The horsemouth looks at Clement and waits for a response. Clement smiles at me like that's that and doesn't say a word.

"Well, Clement, aren't you gonna introduce me?"

Clement keeps smiling at me, not looking her way.

Buck chimes in, nice and easy. He's got a voice sweet like molasses, like some ancient medicine from where the buffalo roam. "Luli, this is my wife, Edna."

Clement clears his throat and I just about start laughing because I cannot believe that someone who looks so much like Mr. Ed would actually be named Edna.

"It is so nice to meet you, Luli. What an unusual name."

I cannot for the life of me figure out what it is about this woman that so clearly reeks gold-digger, gold-digger, gold-digger, but I will tell you this, I am about ninety percent sure that he met her on a flight where she was a stewardess and she bent over backwards to turn him into a mark because that's why she became a stewardess in the first place. And I don't know why I think this but it just hits me and all the sudden I hear myself saying, "Did you used to be a stewardess?"

And this changes the air around each individual into a different shade. Mr. Comfort smiles, amazed. Clement starts to laugh and Miss Horsemouth looks like she could just clop clop clop her way right over me, if Mr. Comfort would only let go of the reins. She checks herself, chomping at the bit, trying to play nice.

"Why, yes, how did you ever guess that?"

Clement is pretending not to laugh into his hand, keeping his head down and smiling up at me through his eyes, twinkling. Buck is smiling, benevolent, not a mean bone in his body, like some countrified Buddha.

"Oh, just a lucky guess."

"Well, that is truly amazing. I am shocked," Buck chimes in, leaving me wondering why I can't have Mr. Comfort for a dad and why I got stuck with Mr. Drunk and Sometimes Speed instead.

The horse lady looks down at me, plotting her revenge.

"You live around here, Luli? Maybe outside of town. Wait a minute, are you from that trailer park across the street or are you staying right here at the motel?"

Clement freezes, fixing his eyes on the ground.

"Dad, we're trying to play a game here, so—"

"Ooo! What kinduva game?! Can I play?" she neighs out, making my skin crawl, the timber of her voice like fingernails on a blackboard, high-pitched and whiny.

"No, sorry, it's a kid game."

Clement still has his eyes fixed on the ground.

Mr. Comfort smiles like everything in the universe is exactly as it should be, now and evermore. Edna looks like she'd like to take this kid all the way to the chopping block. I'm starting to wonder how long it's gonna be till Eddie comes down and turns this little scene of domestic drama into more like a circus of insanity.

"Wull, I'd better go. It's getting late—" I start to move my chair back.

"No no no. You just stay put. Just stay right there," Clement says, reaching his hand out and touching me on the elbow. And then I see it, some little crack in the Wedgwood, and I can see, behind his eyes, deep into the back of his late-night dreams, a pleading from the same place of shame and desperation that I hail from. It stops me in my tracks.

"Well, we'll just be going to bed, then." Mr. Comfort says it, leading Miss Horse with him in a semi-circle and then back upstairs. She follows, obedient, clopping her way out the picture, not failing to look back, one last look at Clement that says she'll get him, she'll get him, just give her time.

"That's not my mom. In case you're wondering," Clement whispers, making sure they're well out the way before opening the cooler and grabbing a beer.

"Wull, yeah, I could tell."

"She's my step-mother."

"Oh."

"But when my dad's gone, she likes to pretend she's my wife." He says it quiet like he never said it before and it doesn't exist.

"What?"

"Nothing."

There ain't nothing to say to that. And I don't. I don't try to follow up or pretend it never was or act concerned or play after-school special. I don't try to do nothing but just sit there.

And now I know the secret of why, even though he's from richville and even though he never had to contend with the stomach-grumbling and the screen-door slamming and the late-night breaking of glasses, even though all those things have escaped his privileged silver-spoon life, he's still not unscathed from those late-night humiliations you might just have to contend with if someone leaves you alone with a trusted uncle or a horsemouth step-mother or a friend from the First Baptist down the way.

And then I realize, for the very first time, that you might just be sitting in a wingback chair in the middle of your mansion, counting your presents on a cool winter night, staring up at some giant Christmas tree that costs more than Jesus, with all that glitter and those bows and ribbons outshining each other under the lights, but if you've got someone, some horsemouth, paying you a visit in the middle of the night, well, then you might as well be setting down in a shack in crapsville, cause you still ain't safe and never will be.

I look up at Clement and he looks back at me, and it's like I met him eight million years ago before time began, and when I met him then, it was just like when I met him now, and when I meet him again, in 2090, it will be just like this moment, on and on until the end of time and even past.

And I could set the rest of my life in this moment. I could settle in and let the dust pile up around me and let the leaves fall off the trees, one by one. I could let the snow pile up and then melt, and the buds come out and turn into daffodils over and over again for the next hundred years, with me, here, set in this moment with Clement, from the beginning of time and to the end.

But that would have to be in another world where Eddie wasn't coming up straight behind Clement with a look on his face that could freeze Texas. Before Clement even sees him coming Eddie's got me by the arm, dragging me out the chair, bumping me into the table and then halfway across the concrete.

Clement stands up and starts to follow. His friends stare frozen from the pool. He tries to make a beeline in front of Eddie, but Eddie cuts him off, wheels around and socks Clement in the eye, dropping him to the ground before he knew he'd been clocked. They are two different species. Someone like Eddie is raised on slamming doors and whiskey till four in the morning. Someone like Clement is raised on apple pie and trips to Crested Butte before the snow thaws. Clement's head makes a loud thud on the pavement, sending shivers down my spine and all the sorrys in the world that I had ever stopped to think my life could be better and that I dragged something clear and kind into a world of dirty trick poker.

I trip over myself, trying to look back, but Eddie's pushing me forward, up the stairs and towards the room. I hear voices yelling behind us, splashing and calling for help. Eddie hurls me into the room, grabs the keys and throws my bag at my chest.

"Get in the truck."

"But we already paid for the room."

"I said get in the goddamn truck!"

This is the side that I knew was coming. Drink number eight through ten. This is the side that was the reason I stayed put down by the pool in the first place. Eddie's got me tight around the arm, making a bruise right above the elbow, finding the last of the cash and the whiskey, hurtling the both of us down the stairs and barreling forward into the truck. Clement and his friends are nowhere in sight, but I can hear the commotion coming round the corner, the boys' yell echoing across the white plaster walls, crying for help.

The last thing I want to do is get in that truck with Eddie piss drunk and liable to crash into the nearest tree. But he charges across the front bumper and shoves me in, cursing and turning red, mumbling to himself about little sluts and being loyal and you never know who to trust. He darts back over, hops inside, starts the engine and tears away.

I look straight ahead, silent, trying to duck under the radar. In the wing mirror, I'm looking for Clement and his friends and Mr. Comfort or even Horsemouth to appear and save the day. But the hotel is dead quiet, as if none of this ever happened or maybe the world just ended.

Because to me it just did.

Eddie is quiet now, looking out into the darkness with a fake kind of calm.

He ruined my chance. I had one chance at clean sheets and kind words before bedtime. I had this one opportunity. I had this moment where I could say something stupid and laugh and feel something sparkly and look across the table at someone young and awkward like myself. Somehow, from out of nowhere, from out of the blue, I had one second to see what it could be like to be a normal girl with a schoolgirl crush and maybe a future with wingback chairs, willow-wear and Wedgewood. I could have crinkled my forehead and studied for the SAT and had high hopes for heading back East to a school with green rolling hills and gargoyles on the library.

I could have had that.

I say his name to myself. Clement. I think of him curled up into a ball on the pavement, knocked out cold. Clement. Clemency. Clement. I make a pact with myself. I make a point of it. I make a date down deep, past my skin and my bones and deep into my blood, into my soul.

See you in 2090. See you in 2090, when flying cars are whizzing by and you can get from here to China and back in the blink of an eye. See you in 3060, when people are made of metal and you don't even need a flying car anyways and you can look up fighting in the history books. See you in 4070, when there's smoke billowing up from the red-crater horizon and it's hotter than Mexico with dust and dirt and a few scavengers holding on, scraping by. And on and on till the moon gives way and the sun kills itself and the stars fall from the sky.

I guess I'll see you then.

TWENTY-SEVEN

Cheapest motherfuckers in the world. Rich people."

We're barreling west on I-70, cutting a swath through the night, with rocks popping up at our sides, red and mysterious, like somewhere in the night we landed on Mars and just kept going.

"They count their pennies, Luli. Don't think that they don't. I know. I used to work as a busboy back at Kirby's in Omaha. You'd never get a good tip from a rich person. Never. They'd stiff ya every time. Hell, they'd skip out on the check if they didn't think they'd get caught and all their friends'd find out and they'd get kicked outta the country club. One guy left two pennies. Two pennies! They don't know what it's like. They don't. They wanna think it's your fault you're poor. Cause that way they don't have to feel guilty for being rich."

I grab a cigarette off the dashboard and light it, peering out into the red rocks of Mars.

"Well, then, I guess you know just about everything."

"Just about." Eddie sneers at me through the side of his mouth, waiting for my reply. "I know a helluva lot more than you, anyways."

I don't give him the benefit of an answer. I start humming to myself instead, looking out the window, trying to break through the mystery of all those red rocks beyond the darkness, casually observing us flying by in our light ship down the road. The sky has a burning to it. There's a crispness here, like it's fall all year round and the stars are made of glass.

I open the window and put my face into the wind, thinking about 2090 and what it'll be like a hundred years from now with spaceships zipping by and folks never getting old and robot slaves. I think about Clement and what it takes to get skin the color of olives, glowing from underneath, like there's a light-bulb tucked behind your earlobes.

"Close that goddamn window."

I open it wider.

"I said close that goddamn window."

"Why don't you just drop me off and then you can close the window to your heart's delight."

"What was that?"

"I said, why don't you just drop me off."

"Why? So you can go back to your rich friends?"

"It's better than being with a drunk cripple."

Eddie slams on the brake, nearly taking off my head. I don't know why I said that. I should not have said that. Not after drink number nine. Before I know it, he is on my side of the truck, opening the door and dragging me out. I am mustering all my courage, plotting my getaway and how far it is to the next town and if I can walk it. He grabs me by the hair and finally I don't care anymore if I die of starvation on the red rocks of Mars. I am done with this date.

I kick him hard in the shin and start to run into the darkness, away from the headlights. He buckles over and then gives chase, limping and running, taller than me, faster. It's black out and craggy and next thing I know, he's coming up behind me. He grabs me by the hair and slams me to the ground.

By this point I am just kicking and clawing and scratching and kicking again, wishing I had just kept quiet, wishing I had just stayed back in Jackson, wishing Glenda would show up in a bubble, wave her magic wand and make all of this, all of this, go away.

Eddie pushes me down and pins me to the ground. I struggle and wrestle and try to squirm free, flailing my arms against him, anything. He grabs one wrist and then the other, pinning my arms above my head with one hand. I keep bucking, trying to get out from underneath him, anything, anything. I see him go for his belt buckle and start bucking harder, anything, please, anything.

He's not even making noises now. And neither am I. Not like they do in the movies. Not like screaming and calling names. I'm just breathing hard and bucking and breathing harder. He's straddling me but before I know it he's got his knees between my knees. I thrash my body from side to side. He looks down at me, amused, like he's getting off at my last-ditch effort to save myself from seeing him every night before dreaming. He shoves my legs apart with his knees.

But I'm not here anymore. I am long gone. I am back in the Motel 6 outside Devil's Slide playing the category game with Clement.

Things you can find in a hardware store. A. Ajax. B. Buzzsaw. C. Crate. D. Dustmop.

I feel a sharp pain beneath my stomach.

E. Electrical tape. F. Flooring. G. Grout.

I feel his breath on my cheek, cigarettes and whiskey, sweat.

H. Hardware. I. Insulation. J. Jack-knife.

He's breathing hard now. His shoulder moving up and down against the night sky.

J. Jack-knife. K. Krazy Glue. L. Lumber.

He's breathing harder.

M. Metal. N. Nails. O. Oil can.

The corner of his shoulder darting up and down. The stars swirling above.

P. Paint. Q. Q. Q.

Now's the worst part. Q.

The worst. Skip.

Skip Q.

R.

R. Rope.

Razor.

He's done now.

Razor.

Ratchet.

Done.

He rolls off me and onto his back. He lays beside me breathing hard, staring up at the moon, waning.

S.

Soap.

TWENTY-EIGHT

Did you know that God lives in Utah?

God made Utah and the Mormons came and snatched it up and called it their own. And now no one knows that God lives in Utah because no one wants to be around a bunch of Mormons.

And I'm not talking about the kind of God who's got dimples and a white beard, like Santa Claus dressed up in a robe. I'm talking about the kind of God who makes rain and moves mountains and lives in the mist. I'm talking about the kind of God who wakes you up at daybreak and says, Looky here what I made three-hundred-sixty-five days out the year.

They got buttes here with horizontal stripes on them going red, pink, beige, amber and then red again. They got rocks shaped like robot giants, with the same stripes, red, pink, beige, amber, standing off in the distance, watching you down the road. They got a blue-sky backdrop with no clouds for miles and a cactus thrown out in front.

They got mist hanging off the top of the buttes, mysterious and eternal, telling you it doesn't matter what happened to you last night, or the night before that or forever back and forever forward, because God exists in red rocks and he lives in Utah.

TWENTY-NINE

I wake up later in a four-poster bed, in a wooden cabin, in a place called Beaumont Kluck's Cabin Retreat. There's nobody in the room with me and I figure out my whereabouts by three pamphlets on the bedside table. The first is a comprehensive guide called "Beaumont Kluck's Cabin Retreat: Don't Tell the Government." The second is a pamphlet called "How to Kill Your Own Chickens." The third is a pamphlet with a flag on it called "Libertarianism: Keep Your Hands off My Freedom."

I leaf through the chicken-killing pamphlet, wondering if people give names to their poultry before they get the ax, but then see somebody staring at me from the other side of the room. It ain't till I clock that this person is imitating me exactly that I recognize that I am this person, staring back at me from the mirror on the wall across.

My appearance is altered, that's for sure. My hair's shorn off to next to nothing and dyed deep black, almost blue. My skin looks porcelain pale and there's some bruises here and there from whatever night it was by the side of the road, all coming back now. I look like some species of alien monkey that alit in the wrong place at the wrong time and got tumbled beneath the wheels of an eighteen-wheeler before a proper greeting.

Well, I set out to make Eddie's eyes swirl, now, didn't I?

I start to get up to make my way to the mirror for further inspection but now there's a new problem. Looks like I got a set of makeshift ropes going up and down the length of my legs and over my body. The whole apparatus is fixed just so my arms can flail around and wave and grab, but getting up is not an option. I go to work trying to wriggle myself out of the knots but then realize that the whole contraption is fastened with a padlock and that the key to that padlock is the one thing separating me from the rest of humanity.

I guess I made his eyes swirl good.

I'm gonna trap this day like a firefly in a jam jar, keep it shut and wait to unscrew the golden lid until all that's left outside is laughter and can-you-believe-its and I'll-be-darned. Otherwise, I'll just be bumping my head into the glass, over and over, useless. I take the day and screw the lid on. Better screw it on tight.

Looking around the room, there's not a trace of Eddie. I wonder if he's gone for good. From my little piece of rodeo heaven, looks like he pulled a disappearing act. My heart skips a beat cause I realize there's nothing in this room to suggest that I'll ever be leaving it. There's no sign of outside life, only the birds chirping and the distant sound of a barking dog.

And now something weird happens in my head where, despite the fact that I got dried blood between my legs and I wish Eddie would fall off the top of Chimney Rock, I'm scared he's over with.

I got this feeling like I need him to come back and make sure I don't shrivel up and die silent somewhere in the woods of Beaumont Kluck's Cabin Retreat. I got this feeling like I can't be the star of this show all by myself. This is a two person cast, and without him, well, might as well just close down the set. And when I have that feeling, that feeling like I need a handout, desperate, I want to pull my skin off and turn into dust. I want to throw myself back to the angels and tell them to start over, start over without me cause you put the screws in loose, you put the hinges in all wrong. But then I remember that I put this day into the jam jar and know better than to just open it up reckless.

I pull the covers to my neck and start reading up on Libertarianism.

THIRTY

I wake up with Eddie standing over me, carrying a bouquet of wildflowers and smiling like a preacher's son. He leans over, kisses me on the cheek and lays the wildflowers across my lap, careful. He's looking into my eyes, gentle, like Jesus Christ himself come down to forgive the Romans for nailing him to the cross. I stare back at him, blank, trying to figure out this new angle.

He strokes my hair. "You like your new haircut?"

"No."

"What about the color, you like the color?"

"No. I look like Elvis."

"Well, I think you look real pretty. I fixed you up nice now and I think you look real pretty."

He continues stroking my hair. I sit, frozen.

"That why you got these ropes on me?"

He stops stroking my hair and sits down on the side of the bed, facing me.

"Nope. I got these ropes on you because if you leave I'll die."

He reaches out for my hand, holding it tight and talking into my eyes, trying to make good. "Now, I know what you must be thinking."

He's got that wrong.

"What happened there, what happened back there was, wull, it wasn't right."

I am too amazed to do the screaming I had planned.

"It wasn't right. And I know it."

I wriggle my body in the other direction, just enough to look at the wall.

"Luli? Luli, listen to me." He grabs my chin and tries to turn me towards him. "I promise. I promise, as God or Satan or the president is my witness, I promise that will never, ever happen again. Okay?"

He grabs my head, gentle, with both his hands and lays a kiss on my forehead.

"And besides, I think you were an angel sent to me to be mine and make things better. I think you were put on this earth to save me, Luli."

I look up at him, smiling down at me like a goofy milkman, lost in love. I muster a smile, trying to figure out where he put the key to that padlock.

"And just to show you that I mean business, I'm gonna untie these things right now. And just so you know, for future reference, you never have to wear them again. Never. Except when I'm gone."

He reaches round his neck and pulls out a tiny key, strung on a piece of twine. He smiles back at me, pulling off the covers and fumbling with the padlock. I notice my legs are bruised where the ropes are too tight, digging in, leaving red marks. If I hadn't put this day in a jam jar, that might just be the kind of thing that would turn me into a blubbering milksop. But, lucky for me, I took precautions.

Eddie unhitches the lock and begins unraveling the ropes, delicate, looking up at me now and then with an embarrassed smile, like he got caught with his hands in the cookie jar. He unties the last of the ropes and puts them under the bed. When he comes up, he's got a little red velvet box in his hands. He tucks the blanket up to my neck like he's wrapping me up for Christmas and hands me the box, sticking his chin in, bashful. What the fuck have we got here?

I open it and, get this, it's a gold chain with tiny gold cursive swoop letters that spell out, "Hot Stuff."

"See, it says 'Hot Stuff,' like you, you're hot stuff."

At this point, I can't even look at Eddie. I can't even begin to start to fathom what the hell has gone on between that night in the dirt by the side of the road, and now, where all the sudden I'm the love of his life, his angel, hot stuff. Seems to me this is either some kinda set-up or he is certifiable out of his tree.

"Like it?"

"Um, I guess so."

"Good."

He snatches it out of my hand and before I know it, it's round my neck.

Hot Stuff.

"I got it outside the Pincus Ranch, while you were snoozing away."

He looks so proud and is acting so stupid I almost feel sorry for him.

"They got wild horses there, you know, maybe sometime we could go there. I could show you around."

He winks now and I swear to God I woke up in a parallel universe. I'm starting to feel like maybe I died out there by the side of the road and this is some sorta stop-off before heaven, some nether-world precursor where you go to get all your ducks in a row before floating off to the great beyond.

There's a knock at the door.

Eddie and I both look, caught. The fear in his eyes is that I'm gonna open my mouth and the fear in mine is that someone meaner and crazier is gonna walk through that door.

Eddie opens the door like a 1950's housewife, all smiles and gesturing. Outside, the setting sun throws an orange light at the room.

"Well, hey there, Beau!" he says. "Didn't think you got up to this neck of the trail much. Thought you'd be down in Reno."

"Headed there."

"How's Karl?"

"Karl's fine," he says, shaking his head. "Well, he's getting a little long in the tooth, so, it's only a matter of time till—"

The man stops abruptly when he sees me, as shocked as I am shell-shocked.

This guy makes you want to run for cover. He must be six-foot-six, and his head shaved smooth, all around. He wears old-timey glasses, with black around the rim, like a science teacher, and he's the tallest man I've ever seen close up, not counting television. Don't be fooled by his big black boots and shaved head, cause he looks more like an overgrown baby or a big retard. There's something about him that looks like a little kid that just got oversized in a nuclear accident.

He stares at me, sizing up the situation from outside the door, his silhouette framed by the amber dusk, behind. Before Eddie can get in his way, he pushes through to the foot of the bed.

"My name's Beau," he says. "This is my place."

No one told him he's in the wrong-size room. He makes the whole place look like a dollhouse.

"Um. My name's Luli."

"Hm. That's an interesting name. So . . . you okay, Luli?"

Eddie steps in close behind him, staring me down. Beau sees me look past him and turns around, catching Eddie stew. There's a second of just the two of them till Eddie breaks, stepping back, shirking. Beau strides across the room, purpose casual, and takes a seat in the green plaid chair, sitting back big.

"So, Eddie, how're things back in Jackson?"

Eddie sits next to me on the bed. I can see his reflection in the mirror, trying to look kind-hearted, sensitive, but making sure to block the line of vision between me and Beau.

"Oh, well, Jackson's Jackson, you know."

Beau nods politely from his chair, stealing a glance at me every few seconds, trying to make eye contact. Eddie keeps adjusting and readjusting his place, blocking us off from each other.

"Don't get me wrong. I love Wyoming. Love it. But every once in a while you just gotta get out there and—"

"These your pamphlets, mister?"

Eddie stops short, pissed that I'd have the gall, the gumption, in present circumstances, to interrupt. He forgot that I got sassy in my blood.

Beau smiles. "Yes, I believe they are."

"You kill your own chickens?"

"Affirmative."

"Don't you feel sorry for them?"

"Negative."

"Do you name them before you kill them?"

"Nope. I name them after."

"Yeah. Lunch and Dinner," I say, trying him out.

Beau smiles. It's been a long time since I seen a smile like that, with nothing pushing on it to make it sneer or fade or squiggle. It's been God knows how long since I've seen something pure without all the bells and whistles covering up something mean. And I know this because it seems just plain foreign to me, like speaking Dutch. Hell, he might as well be speaking Japanese, even, cause this straightforward act is new to me.

Then Beau stands up and Eddie moves fast to get him out the door. But Beau's not quite ready. He takes his time on the steps, looking back. Eddie keeps making small talk but Beau's not listening. Finally he looks back though the doorway and says, "You take care of yourself, Luli."

Eddie closes the door quick, before I can think what to say to get Beau back.

"Shit. Fuck. Shit."

I yawn, leaning down into the covers and making pretend I'm just too tired, too tired for any of it. I fake close my eyes and peek out at Eddie fumbling around, up to something. He's getting up, sitting down, getting up again. He's talking to himself, busy, busy. He locks the door, goes to the table and starts cutting up something white. He's got that bag out on the table and he's gonna make a dent. He likes that white bag cause he keeps getting back to it and getting back to it again. I bury my head in the pillow and start thinking of ways to get to Las Vegas.

"Eddie, where are we?" I say it sweet and sleepy, pretend drifting off.

"Nevada."

"Yeah, but where?" Say it drifty, say it halfway to dreamland.

"I dunno. Somewhere between Elko and Jackpot."

I nod soft, faking, trying to make a map in my head, tacking it up, putting in the pins, straightening up the paper. You-are-here and this is where you want to be, put a pin there and a pin there, too. Plot it out step-by-step.

Two hours later I open my eyes. Eddie is sitting right beside the bed in the green plaid chair, staring me down. He's got the ropes back on. He's got the ropes back on, and now he's getting up, sniffing back, walking round the room. He's got the ropes back on, but now he's got an idea and he's moving them. He's moving them out the way cause he's got other stuff to do. He's got other stuff to do now. He's got other stuff to do, close your eyes. He's got plans for you. Big plans.

THIRTY-ONE

You can count the days by watching the sun make triangles slimmer and slimmer across the ceiling. You can memorize the spider web all the way up top to the left, from the ceiling to the rafters. You can raise your eyebrows when you make the discovery, early morning, that that there spider has caught itself a fly. You can fix your eye on that trapped little speck of black and then, when Eddie comes in and starts waxing poetic about my little angel and sweetheart and darlin and spreads your legs open and gets on top of you and starts making the bed go squeak squeak squeak, you can keep your eyes fixed on that stuck little fly and then throw yourself across the room and next thing you know you're that trapped little thing, looking down at some roped-up little China doll going squeak squeak squeak and getting moved up and down, up and down, and you don't have to stay down there. You don't.

You just throw yourself up into the corner and watch the day burn itself down and watch that pink little hunk of flesh getting moved up down up down and used up, over and over with, and then left alone, all alone, until the next night or the next afternoon or the next set of darlins, when words come out of Eddie sweet, but you don't have to care about that ever again, cause you can throw yourself across the room and never come back.

You get all day and night to watch yourself from across the room and daydream and nightdream and daydream some more. Today I got a daydream about rafters and Halloween and candy leftovers.

My mama, at first, took a shine to Halloween. She tried to participate. She'd buy something, some kind of Sweet-Tarts or Pixy-Stix or whatever was on sale last minute. She'd dress up like a witch with a black dress and pointy hat and paint dark-purple circles under her eyes. She'd sit around like that for hours, next to the candy bowl, ready and set. She'd practice her little witch routine, making up scary voices and different maniacal laughs. Ha ha ha! She'd sit and wait and practice. Hee hee hee! She'd click her nails and re-check her pretend wart.

But they never came. Not ever. Not a knock or a doorbell or even a prank to acknowledge her effort or the occasion. Just silence, like some unknown, unjustifiable shunning. Nothing. Tammy did that for three years straight and then just stopped. We never said anything to her about it, Dad and me, never mentioned it. We just kept it under wraps that it ever happened at all, like some shamey secret we all felt best to just sweep under the rug.

So then we stopped bothering to get Candy-Corn or Pixy-Stix or any other such disappointments. We just kind of chose to ignore that day until we just forgot about it altogether, which may account for why, the one time when someone actually did come round, we made such a fiasco of the thing.

Tammy was out at some dress-up party and my dad was sitting across from me at the kitchen table, reading a shamey-girdle magazine while I played solitaire. The doorbell rang and we looked at each other in stunned silence. Then someone outside yelled, "Trick or treat" and it dawned on us that it was, yup, Halloween and that we were, actually, expected to answer the door. So we kind of shuffled over to the door, side by side, opened it and looked out to find the strangest looking costume you thought must be a joke.

It was this green plastic deal, in the theme of an insect. It had the head of the insect inflated to about two feet diameter and rigged up above the actual head of the kid, making it look like he had two heads, one on top of the other. One human, one insect. This was made double-strange by the skinny, bug-eyed five-year-old enveloped within the costume, unaccompanied, out in the middle of nowhere in the brisk dark night. He might as well have alit from planet Zorg.

The green bug said it again: "Trick or treat," and that sent me searching through the cupboards for an appropriate offering. After what seemed like an eternity of clacking, open and shut possibilities, I finally came up with an artichoke. I hurried back, expectant, with my great solution, and found my dad was giving this kid his shamey-girdle magazine, October issue.

We dropped these treats into the kid's sack and smiled, waiting for him to go. But he didn't. He just stood there staring at us, holding his sack outstretched, looking down into it, confused. Then he turned back slow and walked off into the night, carrying a sack with a shiny new shamey-girdle magazine and an artichoke.

If you think about that, you can keep yourself busy. Just throw yourself across the room and tell yourself stories.

That's what you can do.

I have a special perfect story, it keeps coming.

I have a special favorite story where Glenda comes to me inside a bubble and grabs me and flies me down to Mexico inside her bubble-chariot. We pass over canyons, cliffs and coves with beaches slamming down waves into the rocks, with palm trees and white sand. We alight together and she smiles a big red smile with lipstick and flips her hair. She lets me down gently, squeezes my hand and floats away in her shiny plastic bubble, up into the blue sky, between the billowing clouds and up to heaven.

I wake up to Eddie scurrying around the room. I keep my eyes closed and pretend-sleep, not wanting him to start spouting sweet words, talking gentle and acting rough. All the sudden he grabs the keys off the chair, turns out the light and hurries out. Outside, I hear the gravel crunch under his boots, further and further away. And then the sound of an engine. The truck sits idle for a second, gearing up, then the wheels crunch backwards, off into the night, leaving nothing but silence.

I try sitting up but it's no good. He's got the ropes up, fastened this way and that, some kind of twiny web that seems too thrown together to work. But it works, all right.

I know what you're thinking. Where's all the tears I'm supposed to be crying? Where's all the feeling sorry for myself, wishing I was never born and wishing I'd just stayed put in the first place?

I guess the answer is somewhere between Lusk and Jackpot.

Somewhere between Wyoming and Nevada, by the side of the road next to some tumbleweeds, rocks and dried-up cattle bones, is the person I started out with. Somewhere between the green Million-Dollar Cowboy Bar bathroom and having my skirt hiked up in the brambles and a necklace saying "Hot Stuff," there was a new replacement me put in and this replacement me can perform miracles.

You probably get to look at the world in every direction around you, from a vantage point right behind your eyes. But miracle replacement me gets to look down at myself, over myself, under myself. Miracle me can turn into that trapped little fly in the rafters and just sit tight and watch myself, might as well be watching the rodeo, that's how little replacement me has to do with it. Miracle replacement me could dissect my own insides like a frog in a science class, how bout that?

And so now that I got miracle replacement me, all the things that might be burbling up and boiling over, all the wanting to melt my skin into a dew and dry my bones up into dust, all of the things that might make for choking up or gagging or crumbling to the ground, all of those things that would tear me from the inside out, just get left somewhere between Lusk and Jackpot, hidden in a jam jar, gathering dust by the side of the road.

THIRTY-TWO

My mama had a secret boyfriend. It's true. Tammy had a secret that she and I kept for three weeks and then three years. This secret had parents from Denmark and sunken eyes and a sharp chin and he didn't eat meat, not even chicken. He had a funny way of looking round like his skin got wrapped around wrong and he never could put it straight.

He'd met Tammy years gone by at some dance they had in Lincoln where he'd picked her out of the crowd, just like every other guy in the room, cause she showed me a picture from that night and it was like God himself had dropped her out of his pocket on the way to bigger and better sock-hops in bigger and better climes. There she was in all her icy glory in a sky-blue dress and a tiara, can you believe it? I bet she's the only girl this side of the Mississippi to have the gumption to put a crown on her own head and walk tall from the farmhouse.

She had a light coming off her then, like three angel underlings had been hired to follow her around all night and make damn sure you noticed. And it worked cause that sharp-chinned boy from Lincoln picked her out of the crowd, even though he lived on Sheraton Boulevard two doors down from the mayor. Lookit, you wouldn't drive down Sheraton Boulevard if you knew what was good for you, you'd be shivering in your boots you'd get pulled over just for being poor.

And it was that night, the night with the light coming off her, that was the only time he saw her. Ever. He saw her just that one night and danced with her just that one dance and she got to leave with his soul stuck inside her purse. And he never forgot it.

I know cause he told me like it was a Christmas story, in the lobby of the Cornhusker Hotel, when I was nine. He told me he came back that summer, after running off from Lincoln and turning his life into Falcon Crest, he came back that summer just to find her. He came back and tracked her down through this guy and that friend and the Palmyra High School yearbook.

He tracked her down and took her to lunch, me tagging along, sitting there looking at the black wood rail of the Cornhusker giant spiral staircase, like Scarlett O'Hara was just about to make an entrance and she'd be my mama and he'd be Ashley. Well, that sunk-eyed secret must've liked the way she looked cause he stayed in that Cornhusker for three more weeks and he was just supposed to be there three days.

"Can you believe it, Luli? He was supposed to leave last Sunday!"

And my mama didn't have to walk no more cause now she could just fly everywhere, she could just float across the room and you'd never see her feet touch the ground. It'd be like in two seconds she was gonna grow wings and float up to heaven with those three angel underlings shining that light on her, back on duty.

And then one day, she said it in a whisper. She said to pack up my little blue suitcase with just the bare essentials, just what I had-to-have-couldn't-live-without, cause I didn't have to worry. He'd buy the rest.

"That's right, Luli, he's gonna buy the rest and you'll see now, we're gonna have all those things you been circling in the JC Penney catalog . . . you didn't think I noticed, did ya? Well, I did and now I got em for you, fair and square. Store's open. Listen, I know it's scary but you're gonna make new friends now, all new friends, city friends, and we'll just write your dad a note, see. It's okay. He'll understand. It's best, Luli. It's best."

And I packed up my little blue suitcase and she packed up her big one and we took the 6:15 bus to Lincoln and stood proud as punch on that train platform cause he was picking us up at seven on the dot, don't dawdle. She stands there, my mama, like a version of me projected, with her big blue suitcase and blond hair and big blue eyes made of ice. And we waited till seven, then seven-fifteen, then getting restless, but he'll be here. Then seven-thirty . . . probably traffic . . . then seven forty-five, then eight. Eight? Then she starts to shuffle and she starts to pace and then eight-fifteen. Eight-thirty.

"Eight-thirty? Well, he musta overslept." Make a laugh. Make it nervous.

Then, nine.

"Is it nine o-'clock, really?" Take the laugh away. Take it back.

Then ten.

Ten o-'clock.

And I just kept my mouth shut when she marched into the station, picked up the payphone and made a call, real quiet. And I just kept my mouth shut when she set down the receiver, still. And I kept my mouth shut all the way home and didn't try to make a fuss or chitchat or make it better cause if you'd seen her face you'd know why. Maybe you'd think it'd be scrunched up or mad or mean, but it was none of those things . . . It was like she was gone.

It was like somewhere between that platform and the front stoop steps she'd just flown out of her body and off with Mr. Sharp Chin to that imaginary world with those three angel underlings on the payroll and special knives and forks for supper. It was like she just imaginary ran off with him and left behind a carcass you had to call Tammy that ran on vodka and could only laugh on barstools.

And she never came back.

THIRTY-THREE

When I wake again, Glenda is staring down at me from the green plaid chair, contemplating the ropes and what they mean. She squints out the window and starts talking in a new way. She starts talking in a way you're supposed to say things in church or to yourself or only to God.

"This is how he made me."

And now I notice her hands are shaking and she just fixes them tight on her lap and keeps still.

"Right here. This is how I got made. I was your age still . . . spitting image."

Her hands clasp to her lap for dear life. Don't shake. Stop shaking.

"And he took me here and he kept me here until . . . I couldn't live without him. It's weird. The longer I was here I just, I just. I used to tell time by him. Used to tell time by when he was gone. It was like I couldn't breathe without him. Couldn't eat. Couldn't sleep. Didn't want nothing to do without him."

And now she's got her hands on her eyes and she's just telling it to her palms. Don't count me anymore. She's just telling it to her palms.

"And then, well, he just started doing things you just don't do. He just started taking it out. I mean, you can't just sit there and . . . you can't just sit there."

She remembers I'm there now and she comes back.

"So I left. I left and I knew he'd come after me and I was right. Boy, was I right. He just follows me around now, tracks me down from Memphis to Jackson to Hope. How do you think he got that job there from Lloyd? I walked in and there he was. As fucking usual."

It clicks in my head now, that rubber-band moment, with the beer signs all around and explosives buried somewhere deep under the tree lawn frogs and fishponds back at that front lawn in Jackson.

"And here's the kicker . . ."

She laughs now but this is not how you're supposed to laugh. You're supposed to laugh with your whole face spread out and all your teeth, not with your eyes filled wet and a forehead that says no hope, no hope ever.

"There's not a night I turn the light and don't see him. Every day. Every night. And a thousand times in between. It's like trying to get a hug from a scorpion."

She laughs real hard now, you could turn this laugh inside out and never find the light in it.

"But that don't mean I don't got him in every cell of my body. That don't mean I won't till they put me in the dirt and even then."

Forget about the smile. Erase the laugh. That's gone now.

"I tell time by him."

Show's over. She's got her hands back and her body back and her eyes back together.

"But as long as he's alive, I ain't safe . . . and neither are you, kid."

"Well, don't worry about me, I'll be fine—"

"Goddamnit, Luli."

It comes out of her like a sob before I know that church voice is gone for good.

"How long you been here?"

"I dunno. Three days, maybe."

She bites her lip, stern.

"I got some good news for ya, Luli," she says then. "Believe it or not, I called Campbell and that old geezer made it, kid. He actually made it. Don't that just beat all?"

"I guess."

Above her, and I hadn't noticed this before, on the paneled wall behind, is a tiny oil painting, the size of a piece of paper, turned on its side. It's a picture of that big white arch you always see in Paris, with the road coming out towards you, and all the people walking on the sidewalk, either forwards or away, fuzzy, like it's raining. I look down from the hurrying Paris folks and see Glenda, biting her nails, assessing my state of disgrace.

"I'm gonna make it better, okay?"

I make a nod, but to tell you the truth, there's nothing to make better anymore. There's nothing wrong here, even. Not now that I got replaced by the side of the road.

But she starts rifling through her purse, peering and sorting and throwing back receipts and tissues and lipsticks that keep coming back up, again and again, like they're on an invisible conveyor belt, turning up everything from last night to that last bar to the bar before that.

She mumbles something about a knife or scissors or just something to cut with goddamnit. She breathes out hard and comes up with a set of keys, some hairpins, a needle and a safety pin. She gets up without a word, throws the sheets down and starts working on the ropes.

I watch her in silence, ashamed, not knowing what to say. She doesn't know I got replaced. She bends over me, squinting at the lock, working and reworking, jimmying this way and that, trying and retrying. She keeps tripping over herself, hurried, wanting to be done, wanting to get the hell out of Dodge and wouldn't you?

The lock unhitches and she breathes a sigh of relief, hurried, untangling the ropes around me. Through the flush of her cheeks and the rush of her movements, the looming threat of our current situation washes over me and I shudder to think what Eddie would do if he came back and saw this little set-up. He wouldn't be using sweet words then.

I start helping Glenda untie. The two of us, like spiders bending over the ropes, unweaving the strings of thresh web and then this one over here and then that one over there. This is the kind of thing you'd give up on if you had a choice.

Gradual, the ropes cross less and less until they fall off altogether. I go to make a stand but realize something's wrong with my legs. They're cramped up, slow, brittle, like they belong to someone else and I am just middle management.

Glenda starts tearing the room to pieces, some kind of hurricane whirlwind, throwing pillows and drawers to her feet, before she stops on a dime, the eye of the storm, turning back to me.

"Where is it?"

"Where's what?

"You know, the money, where is it?"

"I thought you gave it to Eddie, to take me off your hands."

"What?"

"Eddie said you gave it to him to get rid of me."

"That fucking snake. I thought you ran off. Motherfucker."

"Wull, I thought you didn't like me no more."

"Aw, fuck, kid, I wouldn't do that. You think I'd do that?"

"I dunno."

"I just fucking knew it. I just fucking knew he'd be here. All over again. Well, fuck him."

Maybe that's what happens when somebody gets inside you. Maybe a part of them never goes out again. A part of them stays there, embedding itself inside you till you can read their thoughts, memorize each and every one of their fears and what drives them where and when, even over the red rocks of Utah into the piney woods.

"Look, kid, he's just got a few screws loose, see. He fucked my head and I ran off and now he thinks it's your turn."

She puts her hands on her forehead and breathes out a sigh, something like guilt and being worn out, something like wanting to take back time.

"He's got plans for you. He's gonna try to turn you into jelly. But not on my watch. Not on my fucking watch."

Something crunches the gravel outside and we both freeze, staring into each other's eyes, trying to hatch a makeshift plan in the silence. Clinging to the wall, Glenda creeps towards the threat, staring sideways out the window, like a gangster in a black-and-white movie. She turns to me, motioning for me to get down.

I mouth to her across the room, confessing, "I got a .45."

She makes a face, not getting it.

"I got a .45. Smith and Wesson." I exaggerate the last part, making a gun with my hand, pointing my finger and cocking my thumb.

She gets it.

She gestures, palms out, eyes wide. "Well, where the fuck is it?"

And for a moment, just a little moment in time, I got this feeling like we're back at Custer's Last Stand, pulling a heist, partners in crime, she and I, like two lone stars on the run, and that we're gonna make it. That, together, she and I can grab hands and fly off up above the treetops.

Glenda peeps out the window, cautious, checking this side and that.

"Kay." Still in a whisper. "No sign of the truck. It's okay."

"Why you whispering, then?"

"Huh?" Still in a whisper. Then she pipes up, pointed, "Cute, kid, real cute."

She starts making a tornado in the room again, rifling through and around and up and under the mattress, the dresser, the pillows, throwing the green plaid chair on its side, tearing the upholstery and peering in.

"How the fuck you got a gun and not tell me?"

"It's not a gun. It's a .45 and I thought you'd dump me."

"Well, where is it?"

"I dunno. In my bag, I guess."

"What bag?"

"That nice bag I had."

She rummages around the floor, finds the bag, turns it inside out.

Nothing.

"Fuck. Fuck. Fuck."

I look back at the Paris painting and strike gold in my head. That was not there when I woke up yesterday. I would've clocked that, first thing. What would a Libertarian who kills his own no-name chickens be doing with a tiny housewife painting of that arch in Paris with wet fashion plates taking a Sunday stroll?

Glenda sees my look and follows my train of thought, two steps behind me but catching up. She hurtles herself towards the painting, tears it off the wall, breaks it in two pieces on the side of the bed and there it is.

The money.

It comes down like a Thanksgiving parade with floats and Glenda starts to jump up and down, up and down, grabbing the money, stuffing it into her bag, grabbing, stuffing, grabbing, stuffing, laughing and saying, "Luli, you're a smart little fuck. You really are. You really are. Truly, truly."

She and I are the heroes of this moment. This is the moment when everybody can breathe a sigh of relief because she and I are partners in crime and we did it together and nobody better stand in our way because we are invincible like Bonnie and no Clyde. And this is the part of the day that you can clip on the wall and march to the state fair and ride on the carousel and grab the brass ring with. This is the part of the day that your grandkids save up for and gather round, jumping up and down like little rabbits, saying, Tell it again, tell it again.

Except that the door slams open and there stands Eddie with a bottle of whiskey in one hand and my .45 in the other.

THIRTY-FOUR

Aren't you forgetting something?"

He scratches the back of this neck with the barrel of the .45, casual, like he just took a class on how to be James Dean.

The one thing we have going for us is that he's drunk. However, insofar as that means he may have crossed the threshold from Dr. Jekyll to Mr. Hyde, this could work against us.

I give him a three-in-ten shot.

I'm betting on drink number six.

I should've never brought that fucking .45. I should've never brought that fucking .45. I should've never brought that fucking Smith and Wesson .45.

If I'd known it would end up pointed at Glenda in the piney woods of Beaumont Kluck's Cabin Retreat, I would've just chucked it back in the drawer and that'd be that.

"You gonna take her, too? That the idea?"

Oh, boy, is he leaning. This may be drink number seven, I'm not sure.

"That the plan here, Glenda? Take off yourself and then leave me with nothing?"

Could be drink seven. Could be. Could be drink eight.

"Boy, seems like you sure love taking things from me, now, don't it?"

But now it's like Glenda's turned into some kind of knight in shining armor, ready for the fall of the sparrow. She stands there, defiant, like she was expecting it.

"Goddamnit, Glenda."

There's something in the room bigger than all of us. I don't know if it's the .45, or the stillness, or the look on Eddie's face, but there is something looming, passing overhead, like God himself is looking down, watching and waiting, to see if this one goes to him.

Then the lamp gets thrown by Eddie off the table and the table gets off to its side and Glenda just stands there still like every moment of every hour of every day was leading up to this one moment, here, where she knew, somehow or other, she'd end up facing down the barrel of a .45 with Eddie Kreezer at the other end.

"I ain't leaving empty-handed."

Then he starts laughing. I mean it. This must be drink number nine cause he starts laughing like this is the best joke ever and high-pitched and he's waving the gun to and fro and laughing again and now he's just laughing at the way he's laughing and he leans up and aims at Glenda and sighs and says with a smile, "It's not even loaded. See?"

And then it happens. Just like that. It happens as if it was meant to happen and it's happened a hundred times before and a hundred times after, on and on, in a circle back and a circle forwards to infinity.

Pop. You'd never think it would sound like that.

Glenda falls to the ground.

You could pick that moment up, hold it up above you and inspect it like a fishbowl, except that it's smack-bang in front of you, this moment here, this moment that ends with Glenda spread across the floor in a pool of red growing, staring up, gurgling, going, going. . . .

And now, in the middle of this stretched-out moment, instead of standing and waiting and being shocked or high-tailing it out, instead of any of that, in the middle of this Silly-Putty moment, Eddie buckles in two pieces.

The bottle of whiskey goes crash on the floor.

It's like some Twilight Zone payback where, by shooting her, he accidentally shoots himself and now he's paying the price, crumpled up, bent, beside her, blithering like a little boy, sobbing, cradling her head and whispering, "Sorry sorry sorry sorry sorry." He lets the gun fall beside him, stroking her hair back and placing a kiss, gentle, on her forehead.

"Sorry sorry sorry sorry sorry."

I peek over the edge of the bed and see Glenda looking up at him, deep into the back of his skull, sucking air.

Going, going . . .

And then another shot.

Pop. Like a tire backfiring. Like popcorn.

Eddie goes from leaning forward, bent, to falling back, startled. Now he's got a red spot, too. Now he's got a red spot of his own, just like hers, and it's growing on the front of his shirt and he's clutching his belly, looking down at his hand, bright red, clutching his belly and looking back at Glenda. You should see his face. He can't believe it. He can't believe it and neither can I and you might as well just drop a spaceship out front cause this moment can't be happening, no way, no how.

Glenda drops the gun.

Going, going . . .

She lets out a little smile, faint, like she's already halfway to purgatory and looking back at this world like a distant memory of a place where nothing works out and dreams turn into sawdust. She can't wait to see the next place. She's banking on giving the next place a whirl.

And then I see him, standing in the doorway, frozen, like a figure in a glass globe with the snow swirling around him and the world turned upside down but he's the one thing staying put.

Beau.

Glenda makes a last stand with a low groan.

Then, with shaky fingers and arms that can barely move, she reaches out from purgatory, like trying to grab his throat or his chest or his heart or maybe just a piece of him. And damn but he reaches for her, too. It doesn't last long. In fact, it goes by so quick that I can imagine myself, ten years from now, wondering if it happened at all or if it was just some blip in my imagination, some unbelievable piece of a puzzle, too impossible or weird or klutzy to have actually took place, these two, with bright-red hands, trying to grab the very last word before careening straight to hell or heaven or maybe just nothing how about that.

Gone.

Say good-bye to the Silly-Putty moment. It's over and done

with now but you still can't believe it. You can look at it later and try to make it go different but might as well shout at the stars, might as well start a fight with the moon.

The floor is made of blood and whiskey and two bodies you can't look at.

Silence.

"Well . . . I reckon they were in love."

Beau says it, letting out a sigh. He sets himself down, takes off his glasses and rubs his eyes.

"I got to Lovelock. I got to Lovelock before I turned back. I shoulda turned back sooner. I shoulda doubled back at Battle Mountain. I don't know why I didn't just turn back then . . . I just . . . I got to Lovelock."

I stay put.

We stay like that for a long time.

Beau stares down at the red-soaked denim and starts to speak.

"They used to run tests downstate. Used to drop bombs and see what'd happen. My mom, the schoolteacher, taught second grade. She used to go watch, bring the whole class, behind a plate-glass window. She said it was the most beautiful thing she'd ever seen. Like heaven. Man-made heaven in the sky. She had me and that was fine. Nothing wrong. Nothing really wrong there. Maybe I was big, but . . . that's not really wrong per se. But then she had a baby girl."

At this he starts to smile, but there's something else in it, something salty or bittersweet, like the sound of something that never happened.

"She was born with her heart outside her body. You could reach out and grab it if you wanted."

The air outside is still. The floor smells like copper.

"Sometimes, sometimes I wonder if maybe that should be an option for starters. You could go through your days with your heart outside your body. Live like that."

Somewhere outside, the wind billows up through the trees. I lay back on the bed and stare up at the ceiling, thinking about man-made heaven in the sky, thinking about Glenda floating up in a bubble and how blood is brighter than bricks.

THIRTY-FIVE

Seems like I've spent my entire life poised somewhere between boredom and anxiety, staring out the window somewhere, in a quiet panic, listening to the wind and waiting for the other shoe to drop. What I didn't know, what I know now, is that once it does, once the silence is broken by the thud of the black boot finally hitting the floor, there's a kind of peace to it, a snap of relief, like the jolt out of bed before falling asleep.

It's the tension of not knowing that gives fear free rein to run rampant and make up stories and make it worse and then even worse, spinning tales of failure and no hope and why even try. It lets it take over until fear is all there is and all there will ever be cause that's what you're used to. Just fear fear fear.

But once you know what it is you've been hiding from, what it is that's been keeping you up at night, you almost want to laugh out loud that you spent your whole life dreading it. You might as well be scared of the stars.

And even here, with two dull red stripes leading their way across the floor, outside the doorway, in a cabin bathed with blood and whiskey, in the piney woods, I know it's not as bad, it never was as bad, as it was in my head, fearing it.

Beau sits next to me on the bed. The wind blows down from the north, the sky turning orange and the moon hanging its head over the trees, turning the day in. He sighs and picks me up like a sack of potatoes, throwing me over his back, walking out the door, down the stairs, across the gravel, and not looking back, not even bothering to close the door behind us.

He's three times my size, a different species, hauling me over his back to God knows where with the cabin growing smaller behind and the late afternoon in front, turning the forest red and gold.

THIRTY-SIX

Two acres down the path Beau's dog, Karl, comes flopping up to meet us. He's a big dog, heavier than me, with two or three teeth left, the kind of sharp German dog that's smarter than most Yankees. I'm grateful for him, sick of silence. Used to be a silence meant something wrong, but not to Beau. To him it's like air, plain and simple, something you breathe in and breathe out, better listen to. It's the words that cause all the trouble.

There's a clearing up the path and the sound of running water. Beau sets me down by the side of the creek.

"Wait here."

He stalks off, pointing at Karl to stay behind. Karl sits up straight, keeping guard. He looks at me, expectant. This is a dog that could rip your throat out or kill a goat, but he's on duty now, following orders. He looks around and decides to make a perimeter around the creek, marking out a circle, scaring off a bird.

Beau comes back with a bar of soap, a washcloth, a towel and an old-fashioned dress. He lays them on a log next to the creek and heads back up the path.

Something in me starts to panic. I cannot start again. I cannot start all over again, with Glenda floated up in the forest and Eddie face down in the floor.

"You coming back?"

He's nearly out of the clearing and in the brush when he turns around.

"Pardon?"

"I said are you coming back?"

"Well, you don't expect me to just stand here and watch, do you?"

I hadn't realized that I'd reached a point where normal expectations seemed strange and distant, like French to an American.

"I guess not."

"Just holler out when you're done, I'll be right over here."

I dip my toe into the creekbed and look around. It's sludgy between my toes but the water is see-through crisp, and before I know it I'm halfway in, washing off the day and the night before that and the night before that. It isn't until I get to the part between my legs that my hand starts to shake. I forgot about that part. I put the lid on it somewhere outside of Devil's Slide and now, here, halfway up in the glistening water with the leaves turning red, it's starting to unscrew.

I don't notice when my hands shaking turns into my whole body trembling, just as I don't notice when my feet give way beneath me and there's a splash and Karl barking and the water comes up around me and now I'm underneath. Now I'm underneath and maybe this is where I was supposed to be all along, with the current coming up around me and the twigs and Glenda beckoning me from the slippery rocks.

The green blue water lays itself out in sharp prisms, slices off the sun, cutting triangles this way and that, turning the creek into crystals, making heaven out of slippery rocks, below the churning of what you never want to talk about or think about again.

If I could stay down deep under the slithery prism rocks, I could stop time from turning and make believe I'd never been. If I could stay down deep, beneath the lost sage tumbling, I could bury that night by the side of the road. If I could stay down deep, I could drift off underneath the rapids and no one would ever know about what happened between my legs with the red coming out and getting two black eyes and a Hot Stuff necklace.

If I could tear my skin off and send it down the river, along with my bones and my blood and my that-night story most of all, I would throw myself in pieces over the rocks and the pebbles and the moss down past Elko through Paradise Valley and the Colorado River beyond. I would tumble over, downwards, in bits and pieces past the muddy waters of the Rio Grande and into the Gulf of Mexico. I would hide myself in the silt at the bottom of the ocean and pull the sand above me like a blanket and tuck myself in deep beneath the clear blue sea until the world stopped turning.

Through the glass water prisms come two giant hands and now I'm up, out of the water, onto the bank. The hands lay me down next to the creekbed while I stare, sputtering, shaking out the picture of myself by the side of the road, with my legs spread open and Eddie above me, on top of me, inside me.

And now I get to see myself from the other side of the creek. I get to stand on the other side of the creek and see myself like a rag doll on the bank. I get to watch myself through the junipers on screen.

I get to see the movie on the other side of the bank, no sound, just the wet rag-doll sopping, some kind of shaky toy getting jiggled this way and that, one arm, then the other, by the giant with the dog, arranging, rearranging, trying to fix. He dries her off and puts her in an old-style dress, delicate, delicate, trying to look away, trying to be discreet. He picks her up, careful, and brings her to his chest. He cradles the rag doll in front of him and walks, in silence, through the forest and into the woods, towards a kerosene lamp in a distant window.

And as I see myself go, as I watch myself go from the other side of the bank, I want to grab myself back and throw myself back in the water, underneath the current, with the water rushing overhead and Glenda tucking my hair behind my ear and pulling me down underneath the slippery rocks, taking me with her, taking me with her, lulling me to sleep deep beneath the deep blue sea.

THIRTY-SEVEN

Beau makes it so the cops don't bother me. He makes it so they think I'm his stunned precious niece and don't know nothing and why bother with me anyways. He makes it so, when their lights come up, red and blue, red and blue, in circles, and I sit in the corner with my hair drying, Karl sitting by my side, keeping watch, that I don't get scared or start crying or make a scene. He makes it so Karl sits next to me and puts him on protector duty while he goes out and tells a story about how Eddie and Glenda were always fighting and how he knew it'd come to this and he just heard shots and there they were.

There's a big circus outside with cops and sirens, blue and red, blue and red, in circles, and questions and more questions. There's yellow tape and Beau outside telling the same story, word for word, over and over again.

There's a red-headed cop that comes up the stairs asking eight hundred questions about what I saw and where was I and how many planks in the floorboards and what's the price of tea in China and I keep my answers short and sweet till Beau comes in and calls the whole thing off, saying, "Look, Officer, she's just a kid, she doesn't know what's going on and I can't say I want her to, you know? I don't want her to be traumatized or anything."

And when I hear this, I remember that there are people in the world who would actually try to make it so you were protected. You'd be sitting there in the corner and they would shield your eyes or not let you see them drunk or try not to fight. They'd say, "Not in front of the kid," or they'd say, "Let's talk about this later." They would, if you were just a little kid, put you in a category of something to fend for, something to protect, something to keep away from dirt-bags that want to give you a Hot Stuff necklace.

And when I remember that there are people like that, people who would try to keep you safe and read you bedtime stories and tuck you in, people who would make you hot chocolate and put in a nightlight and kiss your forehead last thing . . . when I think that there are people like that, people that I never met but that exist somewhere, people that I never even dreamed of, I want to start laughing. I want to start laughing cause it's such a funny joke. It's such a funny joke that there are people like that and look what I got, look what I got.

That's a good one.

THIRTY-EIGHT

You would think that death is something that makes you feel fearful and numb. You would think that it's something that makes you want to curl up into a ball in the corner, twisted up and hanging on for dear life.

But that's not what death makes you want to do. Death makes you want to be reckless. Death makes you amazed you were even alive in the first place. Death jolts you up out of that passing through, that getting by, you've been doing all your life.

I wake up in the middle of the night on a lumpy bed, under a window, moonlight streaming in, cutting a square of light onto the floor.

There is something in me, something in me like a drum beating, below my heart and well below my head, something that wants to take the day's events, the death and the blood-soaked denim, and tear it up into some animal thing, some freedom from the grave and close-call lust. I cling to the bed and wait for dawn.

THIRTY-NINE

In the morning the room is sun-drenched gold by the day coming up outside the window.

Beau stands across the room making eggs on an old-fashioned white stove. He doesn't notice me wake and I stay quiet, watching his profile shaking the pan. There's a looming to him, a dull gloom that pushes his head forward into the task at hand, his place and the day. The years behind him pressing into his shoulders, weighing down on his triangle back, through his spine and into the floor.

The rugs on the floor are deep burgundy, with intricate designs, from faraway places with names with too many letters and not enough vowels. And if you're looking to hang a painting, you better think twice cause nothing doing. It's covered from floor to ceiling with shelves upon shelves and books stacked top to bottom, left to right, with magazines in between. It's like Beau kicked out all the little kids and moved into the library.

He's got furniture that looks like you just got out of your space-pod and landed two hundred years in the past with dark wood, swivels and birds' claws for legs. It's like he stole a room out the East Coast, drove it west down I-80 and planted it here in the middle of the piney woods just to make you wonder. He's got crystal glass animals that catch the light and break it in two, an old wooden globe with a ring around it and wing-back chairs fit for Sherlock Holmes, pipe in hand. He's got a dark-wood, straight-back piano with little candleholders coming out, mother-of-pearl inlays making flowers on the front. There's a fireplace at the other end of the room with a mantel made of stone and, on top, a giant oil painting of a pale, pretty lady in a puffy dress you need a hoop for.

He catches me turning the room over.

"Do you read much, kid?"

"Yup. I got a yard-sale World Book."

"Hm. That's it?"

"Yeah, I practically got it memorized."

"Well, how about the library?"

"Looks like you stole it."

He waits there for a second and then laughs, soft.

"Yeah, I guess it doesn't suit me, huh?"

"Not really."

"Well, my mom left it."

"Oh . . . I'm sorry."

"No," he says, cracking the eggs. "She's not dead or anything . . . she just moved, you know, went down to Los Angeles or someplace weird."

"Oh. That's nice. Nice that she left you all this stuff."

"I guess. . . . She'd like you. She always wanted a little girl."

This stops the air cause we both know she already had one. She had one with a heart born on the wrong side and what do you say to that?

"You could go visit her. She'd like that."

"Yeah, sure."

"She teaches at some weird place where they have huts for the little kids, little hobbit huts and everyone speaks French."

"Well, I don't speak French."

"Well, I reckon that's why they teach it."

He stands by the stove, sizing me up. "How bout I give you her number and maybe—"

"Look, it's okay. I'll be okay."

He stops and stares a second out the door.

"All right, well . . . I reckon I'll just leave it with you."

He turns back to the bacon and eggs, making a plate. He sets two plates down on the table, between two sets of forks and knives made with intricate designs like the rugs. He pours orange juice into crystal glasses you see in commercials for wine, with rolling vineyards in the background and grapes on the table. The chairs for the table are matching with dark wood, lions carved in the back and velvet pillows where you're supposed to sit.

There's a sadness to this room, a loneliness, as if the only people ever here are the people on the pages of those books.

I look around the room and jump back slight as I catch my reflection in the window. I forgot the part about my hair being black and choppy and being turned into a boy. It's an ugly look, like I went from Cinderella to the wicked stepmother overnight. But there's something to it, some preemptive strike against what it is I'm supposed to look like and who it is I'm supposed to be. There's something to it that makes me feel a little more brave and a little less ashamed.

I still wonder if you pinched me if I'd wake up back in Jackson and all this was just some daydream by the side of the pool, with Glenda still inside moving up and down on Lloyd. How can it be that you believe a life that blinks on and off from a lit-up tube more than you believe a life that passes smack-bang in front of you? How can it be that you'll believe a man can walk up on the moon before you'll believe that Glenda flew up in a bubble and Eddie didn't make it off the floor?

These things are distant, you think. These things are distant and don't happen.

But somewhere in America, between the freeways and the Food-4-Less, between the filling stations and the 5 o-'clock news, behind the blue blinking light coming off the TV, there is a space, an empty space, between us, around us, inside us, that inevitable, desperate, begs to be filled up. And nothing, not shame, not God, not a new microwave, not a wide-screen TV or that new diet with grapefruits, can ever, ever fill it.

Underneath all that white noise there's a lack.

Beau finishes his eggs and leans back in his chair, cleaning his glasses.

"Where you figuring on going?"

"I don't know. Thought I'd go to Vegas."

"I reckon I won't take you there."

"How come?"

"That's no place for a girl your age, that's for damn sure."

"Where's my .45?"

"That was yours, eh? Well, I'm afraid it belongs to the boys in blue now."

I look at Karl, keeping watch on the porch, his head on top of his paws, resigned but not skipping a beat.

"I reckon it's best you get home."

"Wull, what if I don't wanna?"

"I reckon you do."

I scan the rows upon rows of books, lining the walls, with names like Bartleby and Metamorphosis and The Age of Innocence. I scan the bindings and gold trim, each one different than the next, each one carrying some sort of timeless secret giving you the keys to the kingdom if you can just suss it out.

Beau catches me lost in the bindings.

"Where you from anyway?"

"Palmyra."

He stops half out the door.

"Excuse me?"

"Palmyra, Nebraska."

"Huh."

"It's not so bad. We got a good football team."

"Yeah, okay. Listen. Two hours, then we're leaving. There's a bus stop in Salt Lake, that'll take you to Omaha."

"You're not dropping me off in Utah."

"Excuse me?"

"Listen, Mister, you can drop me off in Dallas, you can drop me off in Spain, you can even drop me off in Sparks . . . but there is no damn way you are dropping me off in Utah. If you do I'll die and it'll be all your fault."

"Listen—"

"If you do I'll go straight to Vegas and become a crack whore and die in a shoot-out and you'll see it on TV and it'll haunt you till the day you die."

"Jesus."

"I mean it."

"Two hours. Lord have mercy."

The screen door bangs into the frame behind him as he stalks off down the path into the woods, Karl in tow. I watch him from behind and suppress the urge to follow.

That lady with the hoop skirt is still staring at me from the painting. She's made of oil and chiffon but there's something behind her eyes like she just started smiling. There's something in her eyes like she's trying to tell me it was hard for her, too, and that's the way to buck up. She's trying to tell me, Join the club, kid, you just got to put your head back up top your neck and pretend blush and wait for the next waltz.

FORTY

Colorado is split in two pieces.

On one side Colorado is made of piney passes through snow-capped mountains with blond folks made of smiles and exercise and the other half is made of yellow weeds, grumpy clerks and nothing on the ground but a gray tree, one for each acre. It's like God himself put Miracle-Gro on one side of the state and it bloomed up mountains and valleys and crested buttes with wildflowers and then he looked at the rest of the state, looked at his watch, shrugged and took a nap.

Beau drives a giant red truck from the Fifties, rounded off and old-fashioned, like something you'd see in a Coke commercial. He's got some kind of engine in it made of horses, cause he can still get ahead of you, even through Monarch Pass.

He doesn't talk while he drives. He just leaves it to me to look around and entertain myself. You could just sit here and look at the road for hours and pick up thought after thought, like pebbles on the riverbank, pick one up, put it back, pick that one up, throw it back, for hours. I got one stirring up I'm about to throw back.

This one's about my mama and all the late nights and all the jingle-jangle of the wind- chimes slamming into the screen door at four in the morning, giggling silly on the porch. When I think about all the flirty looks at the boys working at the service station or the Hy-Vee or the Alibi . . . the shamey, desperate shaking of the hips on the way out the Piggly Wiggly . . . I would be lying if I said there wasn't a part of me that didn't fill up somewhere near the front of my cheeks with shame and blushing and redness. I would be lying if I said that there wasn't a part of me that didn't have at the bottom of it the most deep-seated, unavoidable, scared-to-smithereens feeling of dread that, one day, that is gonna be me. That somehow, I'm designated by fate to become all of the things that make me cringe and shiver and look away.

And you could be one of those people that sit around, sipping lemonade on the porch, saying right or wrong, yes or no, black or white, and pointing fingers, making grandiose statements about the way of the world, the way to heaven and the way to tuck in your shirt on a Sunday morning. You could be. But maybe you could look at it like this, maybe you could see it like maybe something happened somewhere along the way, something mean and unforgiving, like watching your baby boy turn to ice or getting knocked to the ground or getting tied up to the bedpost for three days straight.

And maybe it wasn't just one thing but a whole lot of little things, strewn together, like oil stains on the asphalt, telling the story of some broken-down beat-up old car, sputtering and coughing, making its way slowly, hopelessly, over the blacktop and into the horizon.

And you could say that maybe even if some kind old stranger came out from the middle of nowhere and gave you a shiny new engine, new pistons and a whole new set of tires, fixed the air conditioning and gave you a last-minute Turtle Wax car wash, that even so, even though now you're brand-spanking new and ready to take on the world with a smile, just the memory of that beat-up old broken-down old time would make you, inside, just a little different from those other brand-new shiny swanky cars, passing you on the road. They might look like you, sound like you, drive like you, but somehow, deep down, they would never be like you. And with this kind of back of the mind, bottom of the belly knowledge, you just might not be able to drive right. You see what I mean? You just might not be able to drive smooth.

And I wonder if now I get to be that beat-up old broken-down car, no matter how shiny and new you make me. I wonder what you can do to me, how you can gussy me up, how you can put me back in myself or if that's just like some dream you used to have about being a girl before a Hot Stuff necklace and sweet words and watching yourself getting moved up down up down from the rafters in the corner.

The road gets icy and it starts to snow two miles outside a lonely little town called the River of Souls Lost in Purgatory and I throw that broken-down car back in the river and I wonder if Glenda is down in there, too.

FORTY-ONE

By the time we get to Denver, it seems like we've been driving for three hundred days past row after row of endless aspens spreading out into the horizon and past, on and on, into eternity.

We pull up to the station and it looks too classy for the likes of me. It's got stone this and stone that and three arches you got to walk through, just to get in. Beau and I sit staring forward in the stopped truck, not knowing what to say. He reaches behind him into the cab and pulls out an envelope, crumpled and beige.

"Here, Luli, you might be needing this."

I open it up and there it is, all that's left of me and Glenda and our short-lived career as High-Plains criminals. Two grand. All that's left from a million miles away before bacon and eggs in the piney woods for breakfast.

"I reckon that's yours."

And I look up at him and remember about all those people that put in a nightlight and read you a bedtime story and scruff you on the head before sleeping. I remember that there are people in this world who would hold your hand before crossing the street and pretend Santa was coming for Christmas. And I think about Glenda looking down from her bubble and I bet you anything, I bet you anything, she put this whole thing together.

"Thank you, Beau. Thank you."

"C'mon, now. You think I'm gonna take your money?"

"Still."

"Okay, well, here's that number, in case you ever need it."

He hands me a piece of paper with a number, a name and a map.

"Don't lose it, kay?"

"Okay."

I nod. I've got that two grand now, carrying it, wrapped up and sealed. I've got a new way out and I can put it in my pocket and keep it with me no matter how not-invited I get. I've got a new way out now and you just wait, you just wait and see how I can throw myself through the clouds.

"Bye, Beau. Thanks for being so nice and all."

"Aw, well, no big shakes."

Beau squints into the sun and I don't look at him. I grab my bag and jump out the door in one move, cause I know if I break it up it'll be impossible. If I break it up I won't even make it out the cab. I'm halfway to the station when I hear his voice.

"Hey, Luli?"

"Yeah?"

"When you turn eighteen—"

"Yeah?" I say, expectant.

"Don't forget to vote Libertarian."

He winks and starts the engine. I watch as he turns down the road, back to Nevada, somewhere between Elko and Jackpot.

Somewhere I saw a movie with slippery rocks and a rag doll, somewhere with a fly trapped up in the corner, looking down at nothing left.

I swallow hard and find my resolve, turning back to the station for a moment.

I stand paralyzed. But then I remember Glenda watching me from her bubble, my new way out, and, like a magnet, she pulls my head up. Like a magnet, she pulls my head up and tells me to forget about Elvis-style cowboys and getting swept off my feet and waiting for a hero on a palomino horse cause he's not coming, no way, no how, it's all on you now, kid, don't forget it.

I walk up to the station and there's too much hullabaloo to know your way round and you could just run right back out and run into the street and that'd be that. Everything here is gray and big and stone and crowded but I make my way through to the tickets and wait wait wait until there's a big pink face in front of me talking.

"Where to?"

"Omaha."

"What?"

"Lincoln?"

"Well, which is it?"

"Well, do you got a bus that goes to Lincoln?"

"There's a three-fifteen to Omaha, drops you off in Lincoln seven a.m."

"Leaves right now?"

"Three-fifteen."

"Oh, okay. Well, okay. I'll take that."

She sighs and I feel like everybody heard me say Lincoln and now I'm just a hayseed from the sticks shuffling. Put your head back up, Luli. Glenda'd have this place cased by now. Stop sulking.

I count out the money, low, keeping it out of sight. You never can tell. Be like Glenda. Keep it hush. Keep it secret.

The lady hands me the ticket and I go searching through the crowd for a payphone. I find one in the back and dial the Alibi. It rings and rings and I'm just about to give up but then Ray answers the phone and it's like the Lord himself just dialed them up to say grace.

"Oh, Luli, Jesus!"

Oh, boy, here we go.

"Tammy! Tam! It's Luli. It's Luli on the phone!"

Now there's a scuffle and too much noise and glasses clanking.

"Oh my God, Luli! We been worried sick. Just sick with this. When you coming home? Where's your daddy?"

"Um, Mama, I don't know where Daddy is but I'm coming home soon. I'll be there tomorrow. Tomorrow morning at seven."

"Oh, that's great. That is the best thing ever. Oh my God, Luli, you are never gonna believe this. . . . I sold it! I sold it all to Lux! And now they're gonna build a Wal-Mart! Can you believe it? They're gonna build a Wal-Mart, right here in Palmyra!"

"But what about—"

"I've got money now, Luli. Hey, maybe you could even work at the Wal-Mart! They got real good jobs there. And when your dad gets home maybe he could work there, too. Hell, we could all work there! Cept me. I ain't working there."

"Mama, can you get me at seven?"

"Huh?"

"Seven a.m. The bus leaves me off in Lincoln."

"Oh, well that's a little early, honey . . ."

"Okay."

"Speak up, Luli, I can't hear you—"

"I gotta go, Mama. The bus is leaving—"

"We're having a little bit of a celebration here, Luli, so—"

"I love you."

"What?"

"I said, will you pick me up?"

"Ray!" Tammy laughs. "You are such a stitch—"

"Mama?"

The phone goes click and that's that I guess.

If I could make Tammy young again, if I could make her not hate me, if I could make us like the people on TV, if I could bring my dad home, if I could bring her baby boy back, if I could hold her in the palm of my hand, gently, gently . . . I would.

But that would be like pulling the sun out of the sky and begging it to leave the moon.

I walk down the station to the bus, idling. It's a simple gray bus, just like the station, just like just about everything in Denver. I get in and it's like everybody's been in there for a thousand years and plans to be there for a thousand more. We sit there, idling, getting hot, restless, until finally we pull out the station and out the city, you can watch this patch and that patch and that one, too. This place is just spreading out. New signs. New stores. New concrete.

And then it hits me, it hits me like someone screwed the top of my head off and placed a diamond pristine in the center of my brain . . . and I know, I know right then and there, that now comes the end of the West. Now comes the end of dusty roads and creaky woodsheds and leaning old farms turning gray. Now comes the end of gravel and hay bales and used-up barns smelling of horses.

And I think about that big blue whale of a Wal-Mart with Corn Pops and Crisco and aisles and aisles of new and improved soap.

And I see every moment of my stupid life, from the jingle-jangle of the wind-chimes to the other fella grinning to the click click click of Mama's heels down the stairs and my dad laughing tipsy up the porch. I see every moment of my cracker-eating, stomach-grumbling, feet-swinging-out-the-barn days and I want to hurl myself onto the ground and kiss the floorboards. I want to wrap my arms around my house and kick off time. I want to throw myself onto the backyard soil and stop the earth from turning. I want to grab each day I burned to the ground up in handfuls. I want to kiss the dirt and beg it to come back to me, come back to me, before that dull machine comes crushing over our house, turning walls into scraps and scraps into dust. Come back to me before the concrete comes bleeding out from the city, past this house and the next, tumbling out, ruthlessly, inevitably, past the plains and into the horizon.

Come back to me.

FORTY-TWO

Somewhere between old Denver and new Denver, I get up from my seat and hurl myself forward past the fat calves and the Frito-Lay wrappers and the chocolate pudding kids. Somewhere outside of Denver I plant myself square next to the driver until he looks up, can't help it.

"I gotta go back."

"Look, kiddo, why don't you—"

"I gotta go back. I left my medicine in the station and if I don't take it within fifteen minutes I'll die."

"Look, kid, you don't—"

"I am not kidding. I am an epileptic and if I don't take my medicine I am gonna have a seizure and oh my God, I think I'm having one now . . ."

Before they know it I am on the ground, flopping around like a dead fish, just like Glenda taught me. Think of a lemon. Think of a lemon. Flop. Flop. Flop.

They are swarming round me now, screaming, hollering, praying to the good Lord oh Jesus Christ almighty. I even got a preacher leaning over me, saying the Lord's Prayer over and over, add in some Hail Mary's. Pandemonium. Anarchy. Cats are marrying dogs right there in the aisle.

We get to Denver in ten minutes flat and the preacher walks me out to the station. He's not saying much but I'm still shaking it off. Pretend recover. Pretend recover.

"Okay, Father. I think the worst has passed."

"That so?"

"Father. The Lord is with me. I thank you for your assistance but . . . God is my copilot. You go back to your . . . flock. And I'll be safe. I'll be safe here in the hands of Jesus."

"Yeah, I imagine you will." He nods, turns towards the bus. And I'll be damned cause he starts to chuckle and shake his head. He chuckles himself all the way back to the bus, none too churchy.

Well, don't that just beat all.

There's a pitch-black bus that says Los Angeles in bright pink letters, like the letters themselves are having the time of their life and you can come to the party too, just get on. The air's blowing out the bus, ice cold. I step on board and don't even have a ticket. Hell, Glenda'd probably just ride the bumper.

"You got a ticket, Miss?"

"Nope."

"Well, you need to have a ticket."

"How much is the ticket?"

"Seventy-five dollars. But it's too late."

"How bout eighty dollars?"

"Too late."

"How bout eighty-five and a six-pack of Coors?"

"Deal."

"Thanks."

I grab a seat right up front and take out the name Beau gave me. It's a funny name, too. Bryn Kluck. 2312 Rhonda Vista. 363-821-1539. He even drew a little map, added cab fare from the station and a note of introduction. He put smiley-faces and arrows all over the map and drew a giant picture of the sun with sunglasses. He drew orange groves and a Hollywood sign and a few stars. He even drew that little school with the hobbit huts and a little girl in a beret.

See, here's how it is:

There's the look-back way where you could think about that old house in Palmyra and want to pull the planks out the floorboards or rip your hair out in clumps, fist by fist. You could stare backwards and want to tear your eyes out their sockets and the skin off your bones, inch by inch. You could shake your knuckles at the sky. You could get mad and say, I don't got nothing. You could get stuck. Watch yourself. Watch yourself. Be careful. Just watch.

You could get mad and say why me why me, you could play that song over and over till you're blue in the face. You could scream at the sun to give you your dad back. You could plant yourself square in the mud and drop your head down and never ever ever come back again. Or you could do like Glenda. You could do like Glenda and put a quarter in the jukebox and say, I'm gonna get myself a new song. I'm not looking back playing that same old song no more. I ain't gonna spend my life staring at my socks, slouching to a chorus of mighta coulda shoulda woulda. No sir. I'm gonna get myself a new song called I'm gonna make something. It's gonna be a hit. I'm gonna grab the dirt and make something and you just wait, you just wait. I'm gonna grab the dirt and make something and make it go boom.

Boom.

Acknowledgments

I must thank my brother, Charles de Portes, more than anyone, as he's the only one who actually believed in me and supported me all of these years, when most people had written me off as a sort of glorified degenerate. Of course, a close second is my amazing mom, Nancy Brazie-Kuhnel, who succeeded in giving me, somehow, one of these so-called "hearts." If it hadn't been for you, mom, I would've taken my rightful place as the second female serial killer of all time. Third runner-up thank you goes to Brad Kluck, who has essentially been feeding and watering me for the past decade. I wouldn't have made it without the gourmet meals, the dumb skits and the vodka I have forever been stealing from you. Now, very special thanks to Sally Van Haitsma and Fred Ramey. You two made this novel happen, undeniably. Also, I must thank my father, Alejandro Portes, Eulalia Portes, Arlene and Chuck Brazie, Lisa Portes, Patricia Portes, Doug Kuhnel, Nancy and Bobby Kuhnel, Carlos Murillo, Jenna Curtis, Jane King, Super A, Mira Crisp, Melinda Hill, Natasha Leggero, Trevor Kaufman, Stuart Gibson, Virginia Savage, Mac Talkington, Julie Castiglia, Caitlin Hamilton Summie, Megan U. Beatie, Michael Faella, Jim Thomas, Michael Solano, Courtney Holt and Mitchell Frank. Ok, there's some nice couples who've taken care of me in my time of woe: Eliot and Alessa Angle, Eric and Abigail Wald. Life-savers. God bless you. And, of course, Simon Eldon-Edington, Carty Talkington, Duncan Trussell, Niels Alpert, Alex Vendler and Silas Weir Mitchell. Thank you.